Y0-EBT-260

THE FUTURE OF HOPE
Theology as Eschatology

Jürgen Moltmann
with
Harvey Cox   Langdon Gilkey
Van A. Harvey   John Macquarrie

Edited by Frederick Herzog

HERDER AND HERDER

1970
HERDER AND HERDER NEW YORK
232 Madison Avenue, New York 10016

Library of Congress Catalog Number: 79-110793
© 1970 by Herder and Herder, Inc.
Manufactured in the United States

Contents

Abbreviations   vii

Introduction, by Frederick Herzog   ix

Theology as Eschatology   1

Jürgen Moltmann
Towards the Waiting God   51

Frederick Herzog
The Problem of Continuity   72

Harvey Cox
The Universal and Immediate
Presence of God   81

Langdon Gilkey
Eschatology and Time   110

John Macquarrie
Secularism, Responsible Belief, and the
"Theology of Hope"   126

Van A. Harvey
Towards the Next Step in the Dialogue 154
Jürgen Moltmann

Notes on Contributors 165

Abbreviations

EvTh	*Evangelische Theologie*
MPTh	*Monatsschrift für Pastoraltheologie*
RGG	*Religion in Geschichte und Gegenwart*
ThWNT	*Theologisches Wörterbuch zum Neuen Testament*
VuF	*Verkündigung und Forschung*
ZThK	*Zeitschrift für Theologie und Kirche*

Introduction

This book is the result of the April 4–6, 1968, Duke Consultation on *The Task of Theology Today*. The major paper was prepared by Professor Jürgen Moltmann. A number of American theologians had been invited to share their understanding of the present-day task of theology in the light of the Moltmann proposal circulated beforehand. Contained in this volume is the strictly systematic theology discussion with Jürgen Moltmann's response. In a companion publication, *Continuum* will present the other contributions.

We hope the volume will mark an advance in understanding between European and American theologians. The reader will note that many of the comments in the American responses reflect a "pristine" attempt to come to grips with a new European thought project. While some judgments seem unjust, not taking into account the difference between the European and the American sensibility, the principal attempt to articulate the present task of theology reflects a sterling commitment to tell it like it is.

April 4, 1968, the day of the beginning of the Duke Consultation, was also the day of Martin Luther King's assassination. The coincidence of these events will always remain a mandate to relate the result of the Consultation to the toil and anguish of the black struggle.

Duke Divinity School is grateful to all participants for their contributions. I myself wish to express my gratitude to all who made our gathering possible. Dean Robert E. Cushman backed up the undertaking to the hilt. The theological spadework of Paul L. Lehmann and H. Shelton Smith, co-chairmen of the Consultation, prepared much of the soil in which the idea of a consultation on the present task of theology could grow. In the work of editing I had the unfailing support of my colleagues Creighton Lacy, McMurry S. Richey and D. Moody Smith. Mrs. Alfreda Kaplan's expert typing readied the manuscript for the press. I am responsible for the translation of the essay and the response by Jürgen Moltmann—whose cooperation and friendship were constant throughout the entire venture.

Frederick Herzog

THEOLOGY AS ESCHATOLOGY

Jürgen Moltmann

Introduction

Christian theology speaks of God with respect to the concrete, specific, and contingent history, which is told and witnessed to in the biblical writings. It speaks of the "God of Abraham, Isaac, and Jacob," of the "Father of Jesus Christ," and unites language about God with the memory of historical persons. It speaks of the God of the Exodus (in the first commandment)[1] and of the God "that raised from the dead Jesus our Lord" (Rom. 4, 24)[2] and links language about God to the memory of historical events. It ties

---

1. The significance of the Exodus event for Israel's concept of God is reflected in the view of the creator as *creator ex nihilo* and of the redeemer who creates new life and salvation out of judgment, that is, *ex oppositio*. Therefore, God has "defined" himself for Israel on account of the constitutive Exodus event.

2. Correspondingly, in the New Testament view, God has evidenced his "character" and his "divinity" in the resurrection of the crucified Jesus and bears, according to St. Paul, the honorary name: "Who raised Jesus from the dead" (Rom. 4, 24). As the God who raises the dead, he is the one who "calls the things that are not, as though they were" (Rom. 4, 17), who justifies the godless and who shows mercy towards the Gentiles. Also here God shows his divinity, his power, and righteousness with respect to the negative, the lost, the cursed, and the contemptible of the world. Through the constitutive event of the resurrection of the crucified one, God becomes "defined" in a new way. Cf. J. Schniewind, *Nachgelassene Reden und Aufsätze* (1951), pp. 120, 130.

1

the memory of unique historical persons and unique historical events to language about God, the one, singular God and Lord of all men and all things. Thus it merges with the specific historical recollection a universal and absolute claim.

This tension between the historical and the absolute is the characteristic feature of Christian theology. In the early Catholic church it took on the form of the dialectic between *Ökonomik* (doctrine of salvation, *Heilsgeschichte*) and *Theologik* (knowledge of God, praise of God, vision of God). In the late Middle Ages it appeared as the dialectic between *sacra doctrina* (sacred tradition) and *prima philosophia* (*Theologik* in the sense of Aristotelian metaphysics). In the modern age it is articulated as the dialectic between historical and dogmatic theology.[3] As long as the dialectical unity of particular history and special historical mediation with the universally relevant that pertains directly to everyone can be retained, that is, as long as the unity of Jesus with God and of God with Jesus can be retained, Christianity is alive. As soon as the dialectical unity between history and the absolute is broken, Christianity disintegrates. One can no longer become certain of God and salvation through Jesus and identify Jesus with that which pertains directly to every man. Christian tradition disintegrates into mere historical recollection and the absolute is grasped in new forms of experiencing absolute questionableness or certainty.

Today we stand in the midst of the disintegration of this dialectical unity. We can relate to historical memory and Christian tradition only in an historically reflected way. The old forms, according to which God was thought of as the absolute, the universal, that which always pertained to everyone, are no longer accepted as a matter of course. The cosmological proofs for God's existence which related God's divinity to world experience accessible to everyone have lost their convicting power, ever since man has no

3. Cf. G. Ebeling, "Theologie," *RGG*[3], 6, pp. 754–769.

longer understood himself as a part of a world striving towards God, but has placed the world over against himself as material of his knowledge and technology.[4] The theistic explanation of the world does not satisfy the man who no longer *in theoria* seeks for the ground of all transient things, but who wants to understand them in order to own them and to change them. The modern understanding of the world has no longer contemplative but operative character.[5] Explanation of the world no longer looks for the eternal truth of transient things, but is explanation for the purpose of practical change.

Thus the theistic, cosmological or, as one says, mythological world view has become antiquated in its basic categories. But it is banal pathos of the Enlightenment to pass over the basic question that this world view tried to answer. Behind the theistic-metaphysical world view, demythologized by Kant and Feuerbach and now by the existential interpretation of theologians, lies a real plight of man and a real initiative to overcome it as well. The plight underlying theistic world explanation is the theodicy question: the

---

4. Cf. H. U. von Balthasar, *Glaubhaft ist nur Liebe* (1963); J. B. Metz, "Welterfahrung und Glaubenserfahrung heute," in *Kontexte,* I (1965), pp. 17–25; J. Moltmann, "Gottesoffenbarung und Wahrheitsfrage," in *Parrhesia: Karl Barth zum achtzigsten Geburtstag* (1966), pp. 149–172.

5. I. Kant rightly says about the modern natural scientists: "They realized that reason only grasps what it itself has produced in accord with its projection, and that they proceed with principles of their own judgment, according to constant laws, so that nature is compelled to answer their questions" (Preface to the second edition of the *Kritik der reinen Vernunft. Werke* [ed. W. Weischedel], 2 [1956], p. 23). Similarly E. Bloch, *Tübinger Einleitung in die Philosophie 2* (1964), p. 28: "The Greeks did not reach concepts of operation and production. . . . Another barrier, in the medieval-feudal and hierarchical society, prevented the appearance of the dynamic concept of function instead of or besides the subsumptive generic concepts." P. 30: "Objective openness is above all also the same as objective changeability, so that the truth of a theory verifies itself not in view of the observed *fixum of facts,* but in the possible *practice* of a transformation of *processes* and their results." ET, *A Philosophy for the Future* (trans. John Cummings), in one volume (1970).

question of the justification of God in the world, the question of the glory of God that fills all the lands, the question of a world which is the reflection of his divinity and which therein finds permanence against nothingness and chaos and thus is just. *Si Deus, unde malum?* The initiative underlying the theistic world view for the overcoming of the agony of the theodicy question is the witness to cosmos in the chaos of the world, corresponding to God, an order and direction of all things and beings towards God, which therefore evidence also indirectly God's divinity, glory, and justice. If one speaks of God in this immediate relationship to the world, he becomes simultaneously accountable for everything that takes place in the world. This triggers atheism which finds no answer to the theodicy question in the theistic perspective, and consequently in view of chaos and meaninglessness turns this world view into an accusation against God.[6] The question of theodicy, the justification of

---

6. Existential interpretation of the mythical world view arrives at its limit in the theodicy question, since the question of God's righteousness in the world cannot be reduced to an existential category and thus also proves unanswerable by an attitude of man. Cf. R. Bultmann, *Das Urchristentum* (1949), p. 201: "This radical openness for the future in the complete surrender to God's grace is ready to experience all encounters as evidences of this grace and has thus also attained the answer to the *problem of suffering*." The insufficiency of this answer was felt by G. Bornkamm, "Die Frage nach Gottes Gerechtigkeit. Rechtfertigung und Theodizee," in *Das Ende des Gesetzes* (1952), pp. 196–209. Bornkamm states: "Only where we throw ourselves back upon the elements of our existence and let ourselves be questioned in the questions of our godlessness, will we be liberated for the discovery that the message of justification through faith alone—alone through Jesus Christ—is the answer, the only answer to the question of Job" (p. 207). Even so, theologically he does take seriously Rom. 8, 18: "The sigh which rises to God from every creature and also our hearts to God becomes a voice of hope and resounds towards the day when the fog will be cleared away and we will be liberated for the glorious freedom of the children of God" (p. 209). The theodicy question is not answered thereby, but rather raised and, as question directed to God, oriented towards the future of his kingdom. It is exactly the justified one, who hungers and thirsts for the righteousness of God in a world of suffering. From the presence of God in the crucified one the person who has no rights receives his rights in terms of grace. It is the right to stand before God (so that one no longer has to sink into the ground) and

God, thus leads to the wrestle with the real divinity of God in the knowledge of the reality of this world. After the answer of the ancient world view has become antiquated, the question still remains with us as long as one speaks of God. After the mythological world view has been scientifically superseded, the theodicy question remains, in its open radicality more inescapable than before, as modern atheism shows.

After the disintegration of the cosmological proofs for God's existence in the Enlightenment, the psychological or moral or existential proof began its victorious advance in Christian theology. As ground of the world, God's divinity could not be demonstrated to man, who becomes more and more the Lord of the world, but rather as the ground and primal situation of *human existence.* Banished from cosmology by natural science, theology now became anthropology. The world openness of modern man who is no longer bound to the environment in nature and tradition is interpreted as openness for God. His question about himself and his authenticity, which nature and history no longer answer, is interpreted as his quest for God. The question of his identity, also no longer answered by history

---

simultaneously the hereditary right to eternal life and the eternal kingdom. Therefore, this righteousness of God is to be believed (Rom. 1, 17) and hoped for (Gal. 5, 5). As to the dimension of hope, we must realize that also faith suffers from the absence of God in a godless world, from the cruciform appearance of God's righteousness, and yearns for the resurrection form of this justice and for its glory. G. Büchner said: "Do away with the imperfect, only then can you demonstrate God. . . . One can deny evil, but not pain. Only reason can demonstrate God, but feeling revolts against it. Remember . . . why do I suffer? That is the rock of atheism. The slightest flare-up of pain, even though it appears in the smallest particle, creates the breach in creation from the top to the bottom" (*Dantons Tod,* III). This "rock of atheism" is also the "stumbling block," the cross, in which God *sub contrario* as the absent one is present. If Christ is "in his passion until the end of the world" (Pascal), the one who believes also retains the question of Job and waits in fellowship with the sufferings of Christ for the end of the world, in which Christ turns over the kingdom to the Father, so that God will be all in all.

and nature, is tackled as his being questioned by God. The objectifying language about God with respect to objects and objective relationships in the world is being replaced by a non-objectifying, existential language about God relative to the non-objectifiableness of human existence. This language about God offers itself as "the end of metaphysics," although it is only the *ersatz* for cosmological metaphysics as a metaphysics of existence.

The plight underlying the theological illumination of existence is the question of identity. It is the question of the justification of groundless and unstable human existence before God and of the justification of God in view of the existence dependent on him. The initiative inherent in theology as anthropology for the overcoming of the plight is directed towards making inner identity, historical wholeness, and personal co-humanity possible. If one speaks of God in this direct way in connection with man, God becomes responsible for the experiment man. This in turn triggers atheism, which does not find in theology as anthropology an answer to the identity question of man, but in view of the infinite freedom of man (If there is no God, everything is permitted. Everything is permitted, thus God does not exist: Sartre following Dostoevski.) turns anthropological theology into an indictment of God.

There are no genuine alternatives between cosmological and anthropological theology (as offered by Robinson, Bultmann, Braun, Ebeling, and others). The theodicy question cannot be answered apart from the question of the justification of man and vice versa.

In view of the ambivalence of theology as cosmology and of theology as anthropology we are referred back to the question of the origin of Christian theology in the New Testament.

All New Testament theologies, in view of the Christ event, speak of God eschatologically. This is what E. Käsemann had in mind in his controversial thesis: "Apocalypticism is the mother of all Christian theology."[7] This is not

7. *Exegetische Versuche und Besinnungen*, II, p. 100.

only an historical thesis about the beginnings of Christian theology, but also a systematic thesis about the origin and the true nature of "all" Christian theology. "Apocalypticism" here does not mean the late Jewish world view or a Christianized modification of this world view, but a particular direction of inquiry: "The eschatology of Paul as well as the Book of Revelation and all of primitive Christianity is moved by the question whether God is God and when he would become fully God."[8] Who governs the world? "For the expectation of primitive Christianity is directed towards the end of all history, the eschatological *parousia*. Only in view of this ultimate liberation one understands that Christ already frees me today, only in view of the redemption of the body and the gift of the spiritual body in the resurrection of the dead can we grasp that Christ enlists me today in the body in his service, only in view of the universal acclamation (*proskynesis*) of the cosmos does it become meaningful that faith already today pays homage to the *kyrios*. The end of history is not only its consummation, but also its key, the basis for understanding it."[9] If we analyze the direction of the inquiry more carefully, we find that it begins with the special, contingent history of Jesus Christ, the resurrection of the crucified and his Easter appearances, and aims at the universal deity of this God. It inquires after the kingdom of the God who raises the dead, on the basis of the appearances of the risen Christ. It inquires after the future of God and proclaims his coming, in proclaiming Christ. Christian theology begins with the eschatological problem, introduced by Jesus' proclamation of the kingdom and the appearances of the risen one.

Since Christian theology raises the question of God on the basis of the Christ event, it asks for God in that it asks

---

8. *Ibid.*, I, p. 146. See also *ibid.*, II, p. 24.
9. E. Käsemann, "R. Bultmann, Das Evangelium Johannes," review in *VuF*, 1942–1946 (1947), pp. 197 f. Cf. *Exegetische Versuche und Besinnungen*, II, p. 75: "That which is most characteristic for primitive Christianity is the directedness towards the last judgment, that is, its eschatological orientation."

for the coming kingdom of God. It introduces the question of God as the question of the future in which God is immediately and universally God.[10] It begins with the real misery, the godlessness, and the godforsakenness of man and the world as it became manifest as the true misery in the cross of Christ. It recognizes in the resurrection of the crucified one the initiative of God for the overcoming of the predicament of man and the world. It consequently places itself in this initiative of God by accepting the great commission of the risen one and goes to the frontline of the true misery of men who—whether Jew or pagan, Greek or barbarian— "all have sinned and fall short of the glory of God" (Rom. 3, 23). Eschatologically directed towards the coming of God, Christian theology raises in its knowledge of the world the theodicy question as the question of the renewal of the world, so that it be recognized as God's world, and makes suffering conscious in the misery of the godforsaken world. Eschatologically directed towards the coming of God, Christian theology places man in the identity question as the question of his justification and makes suffering conscious in the misery of man who is no longer recognizable as man.

Theology as eschatology understands man and the world in view of the future which both shall find in the coming of God. It is a thinking between cross and parousia and holds up the hope for God's coming in the painful realities of this world. It can thus move beyond the modern dissent between cosmological and anthropological, objectifying and nonobjectifying theology, in that it takes up the underlying questions, the theodicy question and the identity question, as questions of the future of God which changes present conditions in the world and in man.

10. Stuhlmacher, *Gerechtigkeit Gottes bei Paulus* (1965), p. 232: "To God's divinity corresponds, however, only a new world in which death is conquered and destroyed." Thus "the suffering that anonymously enslaves the world becomes transparent for (and in!) Christians as the battle of the creator God, initiated by Christ, with the powers of the world for the rights of his creation."

In the modern dissent between historical and dogmatic theology, between Christian tradition and present absoluteness, eschatological theology offers itself exegetically as well as systematically as new possibility to think together God and history, the kingdom and Jesus, salvation and the cross, life and resurrection, the concrete and the universal.

The God of Hope
(The Future as Mode of God's Being)[11]

The first task of eschatological theology in debate with transcendence theology and immanence theology is to define more closely the mode of God's being. Our modern grasp of the historicity of the various ideas of God has relativized the traditional theology of the absolute. The insight into the historicity of man's interpretation of existence has also discredited the theology of immanence (God as expression for co-humanity or the Whence of my particular existence). Since the understanding of reality, in the context of which one talked about God, has become historicized, it has dissociated itself from that which was supposed to give it foundation and support.[12] The "God beyond us" and the "God in us" are discredited, if reality is neither cosmos nor pure subjectivity but history. A different under-

---

11. Here I appropriate a certain harmony of ideas expressed by J. B. Metz, W. Pannenberg, and myself in the Festschrift, *Ernst Bloch zu ehren* (1965): J. B. Metz, "Gott vor uns," pp. 227 ff.; W. Pannenberg, "Der Gott der Hoffnung," pp. 209 ff.; J. Moltmann, "Die Kategorie Novum in der christlichen Theologie," pp. 243 ff.

12. Fr. Nietzsche, "Der tolle Mensch," *Die fröhliche Wissenschaft, Werke* (ed. K. Schlechta), II (1955), p. 127: "Where did God go? I will tell you, *We have killed him*—you and I! We all are his murderers! But how have we done this? How were we able to drink empty the ocean? Who gave us the sponge to wipe away the entire horizon? What did we do when we unchained this earth from its sun? Whereto is it now moving? Whereto are we moving? Away from all suns? Are we not constantly falling? Backwards, to the side, forward, in all directions? Is there still an above and a below? Are we not running astray through an infinite nothing? Are we not touched by the breath of the vacuum?"

standing of reality corresponds to the understanding of God in Israel and in the primitive church. From the God of whom we hear in the context of historical persons and events, all things are experienced with a view to the future, that is, eschatologically. As the God of the promises and the historical guidance towards fulfillment, that is, as the God of the coming kingdom, he has shaped the experience of the historicity of world and man that is open towards his future. The place where God's existence and communion are believed and hoped for is the place "in front of us" and "ahead of us." This is not a spatial, but a temporal definition of place. God is not "beyond us" or "in us," but ahead of us in the horizons of the future opened to us in his promises. Thus the "future" must be considered as mode of God's being. This corresponds to the language about God in Israel and the church, since here one speaks of God always only in connection with historical activity and thus of the deity of God only in connection with his coming kingdom. The future of his kingdom over the world is not something accidental that would be added to his substance eternally at rest with itself. In the exercise of his reign he is the Lord, and in the real manifestation of his deity he is God. Therefore, his deity will only be manifest with the coming of his kingdom. Only then will his glory be visible, and this revelation, this becoming visible, is creation of new reality. God is not the ground of this world and not the ground of existence, but the God of the coming kingdom, which transforms this world and our existence radically. The faith that God is God includes, therefore, inevitably the hope that his kingdom will come. In the debate between theism, which says "God is," and atheism, which claims "God is not," eschatological theology, relativizing these antitheses and taking them up, can say: God's being is coming, that is, God is already present in the way in which his future masters the present because his future decides what becomes of the present.[13] But this also means that he

13. Cf. D. Sölle, "Theologie nach dem Tode Gottes," *Merkur*, 201 (1964), p. 1105.

is not present in the way of his unmediated and immediate eternal presence.[14] His future is our presence, and his presence will be our future.

Thus that reality of the world and man which causes the contradiction "God is—there is no God" is understood historically from the future. The absolute is not, *via eminentiae* or *via negationis,* extrapolated from the presently available reality, but is thought in the category of the coming totality of new being. As the power of the future, God works into the present, for the future is in mastery of the present. It becomes the power that contradicts the present past (guilt) and the resulting transiency of the present (death), and creates, through conflict with the human condition shaped by past and transiency, the powers that overcome it. If such future is the present mode of God's being, God becomes the ground of the freedom from past and transiency and of the possibilities of the new, and, through both, the ground of the transformation of the world. This much about the reflection on the reality of God in the temporal category of the future: the God of the Exodus and the resurrection is the God of the coming kingdom, and therefore a God with future as mode of his being.

If we want to think further about it, we must turn the matter around and think of the temporal category of the future as belonging to the reality of God. Otherwise, the ontological priority of the future over the extrapolations and projections of man which we have maintained cannot be substantiated.[15] The German word *Zukunft* covers two different language-and-thought traditions, the *futurum* and the *adventus.* In French one has both: *future* and *avenir.* The *futurum* is future participle of *fuo,* and corresponds to the Greek *phyo,* with the noun *physis.* In the *futurum* the Greek understanding of being is involved as it relates to *physis. Physis* is the producing, the eternally begetting

14. Mysticism within the bounds of Greek orthodoxy knows the Christian experience of sadness over God's absence. Cf. Chr. Jannaras, Σχόλιο 'Ορθοδόξου στὸν "θανατο τοῦ θεοῦ," Σuνopo, 37 (1966), pp. 12–22.

15. J. Moltmann, "Probleme neuerer evangelischer Eschatologie," *VuF,* 11 (1966), pp. 100–124.

womb of all things. *Physis* is divine. What will be emerges from the eternal process of the becoming and begetting of being. It is the actualization of the primordial potential. The process of *physis* has a double meaning: *materia* can be *mater* as well as *moloch*. It gives birth to and it swallows all its appearances. Ernst Bloch is therefore correct when he understands the *futurum* materialistically in the sense of the Greek *physis* idea.[16] His ontology of the being-not-yet is not forced in view of the linguistic unity of *physis* and *futurum*. They are not really extremes when he lets future and nature fall together in his historical-dialectical materialism. For it is the unity of matter and *futurum*, but not the unity of matter and *Zukunft* (future), of which his process dialectics consist.

Zukunft (future), by contrast, is a literal translation of *adventus* and *parousia*, wherein the tone of the advent expectation in the messianic spirit of the prophets and apostles has been articulated.[17] In Greek *parousia* means the coming and the arrival of persons and events. One speaks of the *parousia* of a ruler, but also of the *parousia* of the gods at sacred places and at sacred times. Also Israel knew the *parousia* of its God in the tent of the covenant, in theophanies and the calling of prophets. It knew the *parousia* of its God in history (song of Deborah), his coming for judgment and for the salvation of his people and his worldwide and final coming in the glory of his kingdom, as well as in prophecy. *Parousia* as description of Christ's coming in glory penetrates the thinking of primitive Christianity since St. Paul. The word is never used with respect to Christ's having come in the flesh, but always only for the imminent coming of the glorified one in messianic glory, so that *parousia* never signifies coming again, but rather the future of the historical Jesus Christ, which implies his universal advent.

16. *Das Prinzip Hoffnung*, I (1959), pp. 224 ff.; ET, *The Principle of Hope*, is scheduled for publication in 1971.
17. Cf. A. Oepke, "παρουδία," *ThWNT*, V, p. 863.

If one takes into account the difference between *futurum* and *adventus,* one can understand why the eternity of God in the New Testament is not described in the three tenses of being as in the Greek eternity formula in Hesiod. In Rev. 1, 4 we read: "Grace to you and peace from him who is and who was and who is to come." One expects that it would read: and who will be. Instead it says: "who is to come." The ontological eternity concept of *physis* is broken in the third part of the formula by the phrase: "who is to come."[18] Thus the *adventus Dei* takes the place of the *futurum* of being. Exactly this makes for the ontological priority of the *Zukunft* over the other modes of time: that the *Zukunft* is expected from the coming of God. God's being does not lie in the process of the world's becoming, so that he would be the unifying goal of all tendencies and intentions of the transient things: *finis ultimus, Point Omega.*[19] God's being is coming. He is not a "God with *futurum* as mode of being" (Bloch), but with the *Zukunft* (future) as his mode to act upon the present and the past.

18. E. Peterson (*Theologische Traktate* [1951], p. 334) has called this to our attention. Do we not find something similar in Heb. 13, 8, where we read: "Jesus Christ . . . yesterday and today, and forever" *instead of* "Jesus Christ yesterday, today and tomorrow"?

19. Here we find a principal difference between the Aristotelian-Thomist God-idea of the *finis ultimus* and the *Deus adventurus* of the New Testament. As *finis ultimus,* the unmoved mover, in the *appetitus naturalis,* draws all things to himself in virtue of the *eros* awakened by his perfection. As *Deus adventurus,* however, he comes towards all things with the *novum ultimum* and transforms them. This is the difference between the "theology of hope" of Thomas, which is actually an ontology of desire (including anthropology), and an eschatological theology which wants to appropriate and develop the apocalyptic thought forms of the New Testament (cf. Ch. -A. Bernard, Théologie de l'Espérance selon saint Thomas d'Aquin [1961]). The latter also differs from the analytical theology of Protestant orthodoxy in the seventeenth century, which also thought "finalistically," but not "adventistically." If K. Rahner in the dialogue with Marxism calls God "the absolute future," and Teilhard de Chardin in dialogue with science talks about "Point Omega," the question arises as to whether God appears as extrapolation and convergence point of all movements in the world or whether one anticipates the *Deus adventurus* in the contradictory movement of the world and thus provokes contradiction to the negative.

If one considers the difference of *futurum* and *adventus,* there is furthermore a difference in the method of becoming certain of the future: the *futurum* is *extrapolated* from the factors and processes of past and present. This is the method of prediction and "futurology." Future as *adventus Dei,* however, cannot be extrapolated from history, but is historically *anticipated,* insofar as it announces itself.[20] The Old Testament prophets do not extrapolate a *futurum* from the bowels of the present and the past, but they bring the future of God as judgment and salvation into the present in the form of the word. The New Testament prophets reveal according to 2 Corinthians not the future out of the trends of the present, but look from the future into the present, that is, from the "judgment seat of Christ," the future of the world judge, into the hidden of the present, and reveal the present. If one notices the difference between *futurum* and *adventus* in the future, and understands the future not as the mode of the time of becoming, but as the mode of the being of God, then there is "future in the past." The *futurum* gets lost in the past. What is not as yet will at one time be no more, and what was does not return.

The future of God, however, can have announced itself in the past, so that the past in new anticipation of future can become present. The "previously promised" becomes present again where the fulfillment announces itself in a new way. If the mode of God's being is future, God cannot only be thought of as the future of the contemporary present, but must also be understood as the future of past presence. Therefore, the future as mode of God's being also contains that which formerly was called his eternity. As the power of the future over every historical presence,

20. In the practice of history both ways of becoming certain of the future must constantly be combined. Only when sociological extrapolations and socio-ethical anticipations are combined, when knowledge is joined with wisdom and planning with hope, social politics can result. It results neither from sociological observation of so-called laws (no determinism guarantees Marxism its victory!), nor from socio-ethical maxims alone, but only from the combination of what one knows and is able to do with that which one hopes for and wills.

God can be understood without the abstractions of the traditional metaphysics of time and history as the eternal one. Therefore, Jesus' sameness in Heb. 13, 8 ("the same yesterday and today and forever") is not understood as his non-historical-eternal identity, but as his lordship which takes over the times and history in order to gather them for his "city which is to come" (Heb. 13, 14).

Finally, there results from the previous distinction a new grasp of history and of the *new* (the *novum*). The *futurum* can bring forth new appearances of the *physis,* but this new is never completely new, for it is conditioned in its possibility according to the eternally productive *physis.* It is therefore correct that one speaks in the corresponding view of history of process in the sense of pro-duction, or e-ducation and e-volution. Future as *adventus* can, however, very well bring something which is principally new and radically transforming, which is neither in its reality nor in its potentiality already in existence. If one leaves the ontological bracket which *physis* puts around history and future, one must say: historical development does not exist. There is always something new added.[21]

The new must not be completely new. It can be preceded by an advance notice, a dream, or a promise. But this new wrestles with the things at hand. It makes what is at hand, what determines the present, obsolete and passing, and in the reception of its own advance notices it establishes continuity. Historical continuity is thus not a given in the *hypokeimenon* of the eternal *physis,* but is brought forth or brought to naught in the concrete struggles of the new with the extant. Historical continuity can only be grasped from the future, once the confidence in *physis* has been lost. It does get lost when the *adventus Dei* takes the place of the *futurum.* This is how in the profaning of the *physis* God must be thought of as the creator of time. The future re-

---

21. That it was exactly Konrad Lorenz who coined this phrase shows that one can always speak of "development" only retrospectively, but not prospectively. Only in retrospect can different events occasionally be linked chronologically in terms of "development." This pertains to human history, but also to the history of "nature."

ceives its primacy in ontology only if it is understood as mode of God's being. And from here originates an eschatological ontology which is not identical with a metaphysics of entelechy or finality, and an eschatological understanding of history that is not identical with a philosophy of history pertaining to integral purpose series.

History of God's Future (The Future as History)

The exegetical and dogmatic problem which necessitates a Christian understanding of history lies in the relationship between the history told in the New Testament and the historical tradition of the Old Testament, between the Christian church and Israel, and in the function of the Old Testament in the New. One can demonstrate in the history of Christian theology that a conscious grasp of history and of eschatology was arrived at only whenever one became conscious of the presence of the Old Testament and of Israel as partner of the church, while the explicit or implicit rejection of the Old Testament and Israel always brought Christianity to an uneschatological and unhistorical self-understanding. In biblical theology today the dilemma lies in the different concepts of history which are used in the exegesis of the Old and the New Testaments represented by the names of G. von Rad[22] and R. Bultmann.[23] Without entering into their conflict in specific terms we will search for an understanding of history that emerges out of the difference of "old" and "new" between the two Testaments.

The Old Testament is not a law book or a religion book, but a "history book."[24] It tells and promises history. The referend of history is not human existence concerned with

22. *Theologie des Alten Testaments,* I (1958), II (1960).
23. *Theologie des Neuen Testaments* (1953).
24. Cf. K. H. Miskotte, *Wenn die Götter schweigen. Vom Sinn des Alten Testamentes* (1963).

its selfhood, but the God of whom one spoke in Israel always in connection with unique persons and events. The Exodus event was fundamental. On account of this historical event Israel knew itself constituted.[25] Its tradition was therefore connected with knowledge of God, covenant, and future promise. One understood it historically, insofar as it established the covenant history of this people with its God, in opening up a particular future for this people. The tradition of this happening, therefore, for all following generations became an identification process, since this tradition communicated to Israel its peculiarity as God's people: "In each single generation a man is obliged to think of himself as though he had left Egypt."[26] One became certain of God, of his covenant and his promise, and one became certain of one's own identity, of one's destiny and hope in "recollecting identification" with the Exodus generation. History, in the matrix of tradition, turned into the process of identification.

Around the Exodus event and within the medium of the identification process, tradition grouped further acts of God. In the beginning were placed the stories of the patriarchs which identified the God of the fathers and the promises to Abraham, Isaac, and Jacob with the Exodus-and-covenant God. There followed the stories of the conquest of the promised land, of the judges and kings, stories which report the testing and the fulfillment of this hope. History existed for Israel at first only to the extent that God had led the way and had gone along with his people in his promises and deeds. Looked at from the other side, this meant that Israel experienced in the words and deeds of its God its own reality as history. Within the medium of the Exodus tradition, in the encounter with other nations, and in the settled life in its own land as well as later in the exile, Israel projected the protological universal horizon in

---

25. Cf. for the following H. G. Geyer, "Zur Frage der Notwendigkeit des Alten Testamentes," *EvTh*, 25 (1965), pp. 207 ff.
26. *Mischna Pesachim*, X, 5.

which the Exodus God was understood as the creator of the world from darkness, flood, and chaos. Influenced by the universalizing of the concrete and personal experience of the history with God, the universal eschatological horizon was projected on the screen of history, as we find it in prophets and apocalyptists. The protological and eschatological universalizing of the knowledge of God are molded by Israel's own experience of history.

The road thus led from the concrete to the universal: Yahweh is God and will be God over everything. It was shaped within the medium of the identifying process of the tradition. What kind of continuity was implied? The history of Israel knows of very radical discontinuities, especially the one involving the destruction of its nationhood in the destruction of Jerusalem in 587 B.C. The interpretation of this catastrophe within the framework of the historical tradition was obviously impossible, since the catastrophe negated the whole event of the conquest of Canaan and, as it were, threw Israel back behind the Exodus. Here the great prophets with their message of judgment taught to understand and to accept the new events that destroyed all traditions.[27] Wherein does the continuity in this discontinuity lie? Apparently only in God himself, who in his judgment not only punishes disobedience, but who also terminates his previous history with his people and now comes as God from afar with a new history towards his people. That is, the continuity lies in the sameness of the God of judgment with the God of salvation and of the

27. In the following I should like to offer some critical assistance in the interpretation of G. von Rad's controversial thesis of the "eschatologizing of historical thinking" among the prophets (II, pp. 131 f.). "In view of this perspective one must speak of an eschatological message in all those instances where the prophets negate the hitherto prevailing historical ground of salvation.... Where Israel is pushed by its prophets out of the saving realm of the hitherto prevailing facts and where its ground of salvation is all of a sudden shifted towards a coming divine activity, only there the prophetic proclamation begins to become eschatological" (p. 132). As to deutero-Isaiah cf. p. 262: "The circle of Yahweh's history with Israel is closed. The exile was in the perspective of the prophetic view of history an end.... 'The old things have passed away' and remain valid only as type of the new."

covenant, and in the sameness of the God of judgment with the God who will bring forth a new Exodus, a new Zion, a new David, a new covenant, and a new creation out of the chaos, the flood, and the destruction of the judgment.

The New which makes the Old obsolete in the judgment of God, and which will emerge from the judgment continues what is promising in the Old as announcement of its own coming on the basis of the sameness of God. The destroyed memories come alive again in view of the promised New. The memories of salvation history no longer control the present, but they become prefigurations of the future which has put itself in contradiction to the present. The recourse to the past becomes, in the present demolition of any direct continuity, the anticipation of the future which in the demolition of the Old is experienced as the New. This entails that the continuity in this history cannot be thought of in terms of substance, as though only circumstances and predicates were changing. It must be understood as *historical* continuity. Because of the manner in which the New destroys the Old and yet preserves it, demolishes the Old and changes it, continuity is brought forth historically. This is thus a continuity which is established from the future, from what lies ahead.

If we understand it in this fashion, new light also falls on the identification process of the tradition history. That process is not shaped by tradition as a guardian or by the heteronomy of the past, but by the coming ones who accept it and personally shape it. For in this identification process takes place—if it should grant continuity in the revolutions and uprisings of history—the identification process of God, who in his new historical activity takes up his old activity and changes it, proving himself as one and the same in the judgment of his fulfillments and in his faithfulness to his promises and his elections. Because and only insofar as he in the future of his new activity makes present his "future in the past" is there continuity in the history of the catastrophes. Otherwise, one would have to turn to other gods and other certainties. Insofar as one, in the absolute contradiction of the judgment, can believe in the same God, is there the possibility of identification. One can believe the same God, insofar as in the different and the New of his activity he himself takes up his future in the past.

Therefore, we arrive, if we want to do justice to the Old Testament histories and prophecies, at an understanding of history from the perspective of the future. History is the element of the future. From the future, from that which has not as yet become history, one experiences, suffers, and shapes history. From that which comes that which was is criticized and preserved. Hopes do not result from memories, but memories from hopes which keep them awake and alive. Historical continuity is established from the arrived future in rejection and preservation of the past. Insofar as the mode of God's being is the future, what is at stake in this history is the history of his future.

According to the understanding of the New Testament traditions, the Christ event, that is, the passion and resurrection of Jesus, is the "eschatological event." I understand the expression to mean the reality-prolepsis of the eschaton: the presence of the future of God in this particular person. It is due to the particular character of this reality-prolepsis of the eschaton that it is only communicated to the whole world in the Gospel, expecting faith in response. The Gospel I understood to be the Word-prolepsis of the eschaton, as the prolepsis of God's future manifest in the Word. Obviously, the reality-prolepsis, according to New Testament understanding, took place exclusively in the crucified Christ. He alone, not we, has been raised from the dead. He alone, not we, lives in the future of God. The meaning that this reality-prolepsis has happened exclusively in him but not simultaneously in all can only be found in the understanding that it happened to him "for" us all and to him ahead of us all. The reality-prolepsis pertains initially only to him. Its universal meaning is manifest primarily in the Word-prolepsis. In the Gospel the universal meaning inherent in the Christ event is made manifest. Therefore, the Gospel of Christ is at the same time the forerunner of his universal appearance, for it stands between his resurrection and his appearance in glory. In that it reveals the Christ event that took place, it is itself the preliminary form of his revelation in glory.

"Where the Gospel is proclaimed, there the exalted Lord in his word on human lips precedes his appearance, there he anticipates his future in the announcement of himself as the coming one."[28] The Gospel is the hidden epiphany, the verbal presence of the universal future of the risen Christ.[29] In that it reveals the meaning of the eschatological Christ event, it points beyond itself to the appearance of Christ in glory. In that it opens up the time of faith in Christ, it points beyond the time of faith to the time of sight, the evidence, the direct reign of God, and it makes the time of faith the time of hope. The manner in which the future of God becomes present in the resurrection of Christ, and the fact that it becomes actually present in Christ, but for us only verbally in the form of Word and Spirit make for a certain "two level character" of the future. The future of God is present, but only in Christ, and for us in the form of Word and Spirit. Thus the Gospel contains the tension of the promise of salvation and the announcement of salvation. Thus the reign of God has begun, but in the form of the reign of the crucified one, that is, in the form of mediation through the exalted Lord.

Since, therefore, the being of God is present as future, but not as yet as eternal presence, it constitutes history as the time of hope. Corresponding to this difference in the future itself which in Christ became determinative of the present there is a difference in the past. As promise of salvation, the Gospel fulfills and supersedes the announcement of salvation in the Old Testament tradition. But as

28. H. Schlier, *Wort Gottes* (1958), p. 24.
29. P. Stuhlmacher, "Glauben und Verstehen bei Paulus," *EvTh*, 26 (1966), pp. 337 ff. Especially if one appropriates deutero-Isaiah's view of εὐαγγελίζεσθαι this particular understanding will result (cf. von Rad, *op. cit.*, II, p. 260).

announcement of salvation it makes present the announcements of the Old Testament tradition. As Gospel it is the end of the law, it antiquates the power of the Torah tradition: one who is justified by faith will live without the works of the law. As Word-prolepsis of the future of God, however, it takes into itself the future of God in the past and is *epangelia*. It takes the promise away from its bond with the law and it makes it present in the bond with the reality-prolepsis in Christ. It thus cuts in a differentiating way into the past and the tradition: it distinguishes *gramma* from *graphe,* rejecting *gramma* and taking the proto-promise of the *graphe* into itself. It differentiates Torah from *epangelia,* is the end of the Torah and the making present of the *epangelia*. The Word-prolepsis of the Gospel thus integrates in itself the pre-prolepses of the traditions. The new covenant antiquates the law and preserves the promise into its own future. Thus the Gospel establishes on the basis of its own eschatological nature continuity with the promises of history. It places one into the simultaneousness with "the future in the past." In this manner the Old Testament gets into the New.[30]

Here we have in an eminent way an understanding of history from the perspective of the future. It is not an objective view of history which would extrapolate the future out of the main lines discernible in past salvation history. It is also not an arbitrary history projection of the Christian faith from the experienced present. It is historical anticipation of the eschaton and herein eschatological reception of history. What unites the present with the past is the future of God whose present form receives the future of the past into itself. For the past changes from within the coming of the future. Christ is not only the hope of the present, but also the hope of the past. If he is raised into the

30. The appeal to Old Testament proclamation in the New Testament is not really "proof-texting," but the appropriation of Old Testament proclamation on grounds of the new event which appeared in Christ and which is proclaimed in a Christian way.

future of God, he also becomes the future of the past. The Gospel which proclaims him can therefore prove itself as eschatological Gospel only if it identifies itself with the promises of the past. The understanding of history as future in the past, in the present turns into historical initiative, that is, into eschatological mission among Jews and heathens. One gets an idea of the future in the past from the eschatological initiative in the present in favor of the universal future, as St. Paul interprets it in Rom. 9–11. Herein the place of the Gospel and faith is not usurped by a concept of history, but Gospel and faith arrive at their historical self-consciousness.

God and Jesus—The Advent of God's Future

The hinge of history (Michalson) for a Christian understanding of history lies in Jesus Christ himself. Jesus identified the eschatological kingdom of God with his Word, his activity, and his suffering, and thus with his person. The kingdom of God has identified itself with Jesus in the resurrection of the crucified one. In his words and deeds Jesus has anticipated the kingdom of God and has opened the coming of the kingdom. In the resurrection from the dead God has anticipated in this *one* his kingdom of "life from the dead," and has herein, through this *one,* opened the future of the resurrection and the life.

The plot of historicity and absoluteness, of history and eschatology, of the concrete and the universal thickens at this point as the question of the identity of the risen one with the crucified one. Through his death Jesus became historical. Through his resurrection he became eschatological. He became the coming Lord who mediates the future of God. God's future which received the crucified one thus assumes its real mediating form in the reign of the crucified one. A Christian understanding of history in its core must therefore be developed out of Christology, because the problem of how the experience of the double ending of Jesus' life—out of life into death and out of death into life, experienced in his crucifixion and in the appearances of the exalted one—could find a common denominator is a Christological problem. Therefore, we cannot apply to Jesus Christ a concept of history that has been arrived at in terms of other experiences. But we must develop from his identity in the absolute difference of cross and resurrection a Christological concept of history which can come to grips with other experiences of history.[31]

(A) *Jesus the Lord*

In what way does God identify himself with Jesus and his destiny (*Geschick*)? God identifies himself with Jesus by receiving the crucified one into his future as mode of his being. If we start with the resurrection, we must say that God in his being does not become identical with Jesus, but identifies with Jesus through an act of his will. God has offered him up to a death at the cross of forsakenness. God has raised him from the dead and exalted him to be the Lord of his coming kingdom. In passion and resurrection God acts in Jesus. If one calls passion and resurrection the "Christ event," it is God who is the Subject of this event. Consequently, in the New Testament one differentiates between God and Jesus, the Lord. God is adored, but the Lord is called upon. This differentiation is based on a clear definition of the relationship between God and the *Kyrios:* through him we have access to God, in his name we can pray to God.[32] In Pauline Christology this differentiation emerges in his kingdom theology (1 Cor. 15, 23 ff.). God

---

31. This had already been attempted by Richard R. Niebuhr (*Resurrection and Historical Reason* [1957]), even though more in debate with modern historiography than in a new Christology.

32. Following E. Käsemann, *op. cit.*, II, p. 127; also H. Conzelmann, "Christus im Gottesdienst der neutestamentlichen Zeit," *MPTh*, 55 (1966), p. 361.

has delegated his *basileia* to Jesus for a definite purpose and a definite time, that is, for the time from his exaltation until the consummation of his work of salvation. At this time, Jesus will deliver the kingdom to God the Father, so that God will be all in all. The reign of the crucified one, as it becomes known in the Christological titles, is a delegated reign (*Lehnsherrschaft*). It is limited and preliminary. "It solely serves the purpose to make room for the sovereign reign of God."[33] Christ is "God's stand-in" (Käsemann), the "Lieutenant de Dieu" (Calvin),[34] "God's deputy,"[35] over against a world which is not fully subjected to God. Christ's reign, specifically, is the realization of God's dominion over the world in view of the captivity of the world to sin, death, and the devil (the moral, physical, and metaphysical evil). It is, therefore, the reign of the crucified one. The eschatological liberation of the world has begun through Easter and we look forward to its victorious culmination.

If one would measure the New Testament by the criterion of church dogma, its Christology (this pertains to all types within the New Testament) would have to be called subordinationist.[36] To be more precise, it is in this respect an "eschatological subordinationism."[37] We thus find in Christology again the two-level character of God's future: the reign of the crucified one is the mediation of the immediate dominion of God in a godless and godforsaken world.[38] The immediate dominion of God which de-

---

33. E. Käsemann, *op. cit.*, p. 280.
34. As to Calvin's Christology in this question cf. W. Kratz, "Christus —Gott und Mensch," *EvTh*, 19 (1959), pp. 209–219; and as regards an excessive consequence of Calvin's Christology, A. A. van Ruler, *Gestaltwerdung Christi in der Welt* (1956).
35. D. Sölle, *Stellvertretung. Ein Kapitel Theologie nach dem "Tode Gottes"* (1965).
36. H. Conzelmann, *op. cit.*, p. 362.
37. E. Brunner, *Das Ewige als Zukunft und Gegenwart* (1965), p. 227.
38. H. Conzelmann, *op. cit.*, p. 362: "Christ's reign, technically put, is the realization of God's sovereignty over the world in view of the revolt of the world, of sin, and of death."

stroys death and transforms faith into sight is the "inner future" of the present reign of Christ. Communion with God is only found in communion with Christ. The reign of Christ is characterized by the fact that only he, but not we, has been wrested from death. It is limited by his resurrection as the *terminus a quo* and our resurrection as the *terminus ad quem*.[39] It is, therefore, not ontologically determined through Jesus' being, but functionally through his serving and reigning for God. The New Testament titles of Christ characterize functions and are not yet qualifications of being.

(B) *Jesus the Son of God*

The eschatological subordinationism in Christology only results, however, if one one-sidedly looks from the presence of Christ upon the future of God and considers his present function merely in view of its goal and purpose. If, conversely, one looks from the future of God to the presence of Christ, the subordinationist and functional definitions of Christology do not suffice. One can clarify this with respect to the goal of mediation where the mediator's work becomes unnecessary. Here already Calvin's Christology got lost in the dark. Even more visibly, the modern subordinationist Christologies move towards the absurd at this point. As "stand-in," "deputy," "mandator," and "functionary" of God, Christ must disappear and "dissolve" himself as soon as God comes in his complete reign. The mediating reign of Christ is not significant in itself. It only mediates the changeover in government from the kingdom of sin to the kingdom of God. It represents God only until God comes. It is only an "emergency solution" of God which is necessitated by the world's predicament in sin.[40]

39. E. Käsemann, *op. cit.*, II, p. 128.
40. Among the Christological functionalists, most clearly A. A. van Ruler, *op. cit.*, p. 34. Thus he demands: "Over against Barth one should

But this is not at all the New Testament understanding of Christology and eschatology. According to 1 Cor. 15, 28, Jesus will turn over the kingdom not just to "God," but to "God, the Father." God, however, becomes manifest as "Father" in the obedience of the "Son." Consequently, we have in the obedience of the Son not merely a functional mediation of the coming sovereign reign of God, but also the reign of God in the love of the Father himself. Not only did God offer up Jesus as medium for the realization of his coming kingdom, but Jesus has also offered up himself and is one with the Father in his self-giving. In the obedience of the Son, therefore, we find the true image of God and not only a mediation that would become superfluous. The trinitarian relationship of the Father to the Son becomes the permanent characteristic of God. It is the inner rationale of Christ's reign. Christ thus reigns not only for God and in God's place until God himself takes his place, but God reigns already in Christ. Jesus is not only the "stand-in" of God's future, but conversely also the incarnation of God's future. He is not only the forerunner of the future of God, but also its realization. He is not only the mediator of a new life from God, but also becomes its foundation. This new life cannot bypass Christ. It owes itself eternally to "the Lamb that was slain." The thought of a mediator who becomes unnecessary drives an eschatological Christology to the absurd. The eschatological difference between Jesus the Lord and the deity of God (in the reality-prolepsis) can be

---

view creation, in my opinion, by itself and not mix anything of Christ, the Son of God in the flesh, into it. One should also over against the entire Christian tradition keep apart the kingdom of glory and not mix anything of Christ into it. The *assumptio carnis,* the assumption of the flesh is necessary only because of sin. In the last judgment the *crisis* also enters into sin and undoes it. The cover of the flesh, the specific form of God in Christ, will then be put aside." Similarly D. Sölle, *op. cit.,* p. 201: "Christ guards the unforgotten kingdom and enables us to live in waiting. Herein he remains unsurpassed. There is no greater closeness to God than is his, that is, that of the protagonist and the stand-in, of the lawyer and the actor. He is surpassed only by the new heaven and the new earth for which we wait."

thought of meaningfully only on the basis of God's identification with Jesus, of the Father with the Son.

1. In Jesus' cross and resurrection God not only acts as the Lord, but also suffers as Father in offering up his Son. The Christ event is not only an action of God's superiority over death, but also in the self-giving of the Son an action of the love of God the Father. Through the obedience of the Son in the suffering of his love God wins back his world, not through a new dictatorship. Therefore, Christ does not merely mediate a changeover of "government" from the dictatorship of sin to the dictatorship of God's justice, although St. Paul occasionally uses similar phrases as, for example, in Rom. 6, 16 ff. Even so, he narrows down the parallel: "I am speaking to you in human terms, because of your natural limitations." As Christ and God's righteousness take the place of evil and the power of sin, there is not only a change in government, but also in the form of government. Sin and death reign in terms of *ananke*. But Christ wins out through suffering love, and he reigns in the brotherhood of the children of God (Rom. 8, 28) through freedom. In the place of the dictatorship of sin and death we now have the brotherly "democracy" of the Spirit in which the firstborn among many brethren conforms to humankind. It is exactly this obedience of Christ to his Father which fulfills itself (according to 1 Cor. 15) in the transfer of the kingdom to the Pantokrator, so that God will not only be all in all, but also Father of all who are called children in heaven and on earth. The "changeover of government" does not take place as an exchange of dictators, but as the "joyous change" in the justification of the sinner through the righteous one who has been made sin for us.[41]

---

41. I offer this as critical observation over against the altogether too synonymous use of "government" and "changeover of government" in the theology of E. Käsemann.

2. If Christ would be only the substitute and "stand-in" of God and his creature, the end for which he works and at which he would make himself unnecessary would be the *restitutio in integrum,* the restitution of the good old creation. He would bring nothing new into history, but would only eliminate the fall from the good old origin. The kingdom of glory would thus be nothing but the good old creation. But this is not at all the view of the New Testament. The hope of faith in Christ expects more of the end than there was in the beginning. The new that has come into the world through Christ is the Fatherhood of God and the sonship of the believer. The new creation and the new heaven and the new earth are much more than the old creation and also more than the restitution of the old creation. It was exactly the apocalyptic theology of the New Testament which developed that knowledge of the new which is not only new as compared with sin, but also as compared with creation. In Christian theology this knowledge was preserved by Irenaeus (*imago Dei—similitudo Dei*), Athanasius (*theopoiesis*), Augustine (*non posse peccare, non posse mori*), Osiander, and Karl Barth.

If Christ is God's emergency act of grace in view of the plight of sin, this act, however, does not find its criterion in the measure of sin, but in the future of new life that God wants to create. It is this new reality of God's future which lies in the sonship of the Son, in the free sonship of the believers in communion with him, and in the glorification of the transient world. This future is the inner substance of the historical mediation between God and man in Jesus Christ. It is presence of the future which arrives in the historical mediation of the future in Christ. Thus Christians do not wait solely for the kingdom of God which Christ mediates, but also for the parousia of Christ himself. For their new life is hidden in him and can therefore become manifest only in his manifestation. The parousia of Christ brings the believers sight, manifests the deity of the Father, and brings the world to its goal.

(C) *The Meaning of the Cross of the Risen Christ*

Eschatological Christology which does not find the turn to Christological eschatology misses the meaning of the cross, for it looks merely to the anticipation of the future in the Christ event, but not conversely also upon the incarnation of the future of the kingdom in the Christ event. It looks from the history of Christ towards the future of God, but not from the future of God towards the history of Christ. It is, however, not only "one" who has been raised from the dead as the prolepsis of the future of all, as the proleptic titles of Christ indicate, "the first fruits of those who have fallen asleep" (1 Cor. 15, 20), "the Author of life," (Acts 3, 15), "the firstborn among many brethren" (Rom. 8, 29), and so forth, but *this particular* one, "the crucified one." The answer to the question of the delay of the parousia—why only this one and not also all the others at the same time, why "at first" Christ and not total salvation at once?—can only be found in a development of the meaning of his cross.

The Christ who is "in front" of us and who goes "ahead of us" in the glory of the coming God through his suffering and death on the cross becomes the Christ who died "for us" and to our advantage. The meaning of the prolepsis of the eschaton in him can only be grasped in his "pro-existence" for us. The resurrection faith on the basis of the Easter appearances of Christ can only be retained *as faith in the cross* if it does not want to disintegrate in enthusiasm. Only through the deeper insight into the meaning of his suffering on the cross did the direct "present tense" eschatology of the Easter and Spirit experiences in the primitive church turn into Christological eschatology which finds resurrection and life mediated through the suffering and death of Christ.[42] The understanding of the reality-prolepsis

---
42. Cf. H. W. Bartsch, *Das Auferstehungszeugnis. Sein historisches und sein theologisches Problem* (1965).

of the eschaton does indeed emerge from the theology of Easter. But if the whole Christ event (passion and resurrection) is to be sufficiently represented, the theology of Easter must be broadened by a theology of the cross. One must develop the concept of prolepsis from the concept of substitution, so that it becomes clear that God for this reason anticipates his future of resurrection and life in this particular one in order to mediate it to us through him.[43] The manner in which God mediates his future through this particular one is the form of substitutionary suffering, sacrificial death, and accepting love. If one looks from the future of God into the godless and godforsaken present, the cross of Christ becomes the present form of the resurrection. The cross is the negative form of the kingdom of God, and the kingdom of God is the positive content of the cross.[44]

While the Easter faith was a fixed factor for the primitive church, the interpretations of the cross were apparently varied, for his death on the cross was a painful riddle. Without getting involved in the problem of the process of the tradition in the primitive church as regards the meaning of Jesus' death, the question arises whether this meaning is adequately understood today: (a) if his death is seen in the context of his life and actions (the theology of the quest of the historical Jesus), (b) if his resurrection is understood as the significance of the death (dialectical theology), and (c) if only his resurrection, but not his cross, is seen in the eschatological context (apocalyptic theology). If we place his cross together with his resurrection into the eschatological expectation of the future of God, his death

---

43. It seems a lacuna in the magnificent volume of W. Pannenberg, *Grundzüge der Christologie* (1964), that it does not quite integrate the truth of the *theologia crucis* into its Christology of the resurrection, and thus does not avail itself of Christ's death on the cross for the interpretation of his resurrection while deriving the death from general human relationships of substitution.

44. G. W. F. Hegel, *Philosophie der Religion* (ed. H. Glockner), *Werke,* 16:2, p. 299.

on the cross must be understood as the anticipation of the final judgment of God in everything that contradicts him. Thus Mark depicted the passion in apocalyptic colors, and St. Paul understood the cross as execution of the approaching wrath of God over the totality of the fallen creation. Good Friday is not merely the individual Good Friday, but the "speculative Good Friday" (that is, the Good Friday understood in the context of the whole of creation)[45] of the execution of the wrath of God over everything that cannot last on its own grounds in view of the future of God. His cross is the prolepsis of the *annihilatio mundi,* the vanishing of the world in nothingness.

If God, however, has raised this one, who had been "offered up," from the death of godforsakenness, life and lasting reality have appeared in the one who was offered up for all. Therefore, the godless find in him God's righteousness, and God's enemies reconciliation, and the believers "new creation." If we in this way understand the cross apocalyptically, the power of his suffering and the fruit of his death serve Christ's resurrection and God's new creation. Herein it finds its universal significance for all sinners who lack the glory of God. But this means, conversely: if resurrection took place in this crucified one, resurrection and life thus arrive here only in the power of his suffering and the fruit of his death, as justification of the godless and reconciliation of the enemies. The historical mediation of salvation happens in the solidarity of the one who brings salvation with those who lack salvation and in his substitutionary suffering and death for them. The cross of Christ modifies the prolepsis of eternal life under the conditions of death in order to bring redemption from these conditions. It modifies the prolepsis of God's justification under the conditions of sin for the justification of sinners. That is, it brings the future of God's kingdom into the presence of sin, death, and devil through substitutionary suffering. It brings God's coming freedom and peace into a hostile

---

45. G. W. F. Hegel, *Glauben und Wissen* (PhB, 626, 1928), p. 124.

world through self-renouncing love. It reigns through service. The prolepsis of the future of salvation is revealed in the "*pro nobis*" character of Christ's death. Christ's cross gains significance if one understands it as "the cross of the risen one." Christian eschatology is, therefore, *eschatologia crucis,* that is, a hope for God's future and his kingdom which depends on Christ's suffering and death, since it recognizes herein the groundless proof of God's faithfulness, the love of God hoping for the future of man, as it were. Therefore, in the anticipation of the resurrection in Christ lies also the grace of the coming towards us (*Zuvorkommenheit*) of God, who retains for man in the image of the resurrected one his future of salvation, whereas in the cross of Christ he has taken care of man's past (guilt) and transiency (death). Therefore, man, who has lost his future and glory before God, finds only in communion with the suffering of Christ the future of the resurrection (Phil. 3, 10–12).

In the *anticipation* of God's future in Christ we thus have the grace of God's coming towards us. Here God's kingdom in the context of the world of sin and death is realized in a liberation through substitution. Viewed from the "hither" side of the future, Christ's cross therefore is the *incarnation* of his resurrection and of life, for it is the reality-mediation of God's future for the godless who are without future. He who was raised "before" us becomes our mediator. He "takes our place" for the sake of our true future. He becomes present and past in order that we become men of the future and the present. In the prolepsis inherent in the Christ event, therefore, lies the making present of our future under the conditions of estrangement in which we live. Conversely, the ontological priority of the future of God means not that God is our utopia, but that we are God's "utopia." We are hoping for God, because he hopes for us. Since Christ intercedes "for us" and is "with us," we are already what we will be, "in him" (new creation), and we will be what we are in him "with him" in his future. We will "reign with him," "become manifest with him," and "will be glorified with him."

We believe in God because God believes in us and the world.[46] God has made himself in Christ for us our "creditor." This interceding of God for us can only be grasped by us in faith. But if this interceding of God for us and to our advantage is standing in the horizon of his future, our faith thus inevitably also stands in the horizon of hope. The making present of the coming God in Christ's substitution creates faith in us. The making present of the coming God in the resurrection of Christ creates hope in us. Thus faith has the *prius,* since it is the first thing that corresponds in us to God's future. But hope owns the primacy, since in faith everything is directed to God's future and faith owes itself to the opening up of this future. In faith hope finds its ground in Christ's cross. In hope faith finds its end in Christ's parousia. What is grounded on faith and becomes effective through hope is love. It is the new being and the resurrection life under the conditions of transiency and death.

(D) *Resurrection and Mission*

Having interpreted Jesus' cross as reality-mediation in the light of the proleptic understanding of his resurrection, we must now turn to the mode of the universal mediation of the eschatological future-mediation. Earlier, we described the word of the Gospel as Word-prolepsis. This concept must be deepened in terms of Word-mediation. Resurrection and life are real in the power of Christ's suffering and in the fruit of his dying. The significance of the Christ event in general in the history before the eschaton is mediated through the Word and Spirit of mission. The Easter appearances of the resurrected one not only illuminate in

---

46. I am using here a formulation of G. Gloege, *Gnade für die Welt* (1964), p. 22.

retrospect the meaning of the cross, but also in prospect the way in which the reality-anticipation of the future comes into the world.[47] All Easter appearances are simultaneously *Berufungsvisionen,* and contain the commission and the calling for the apostolate. This is the meaning of the abbreviating phrase: Christ rose into the kerygma. The present reality of the resurrection is the Gospel and the Spirit, who moves the Gospel. In everything *what* the Gospel says, it is revelation and manifestation of the future of God in Christ. In the fact, however, *that* it says this and puts it into a Word to Jews and Gentiles, it is Word-prolepsis of the glorification of Christ.

The Gospel contains in itself promise of salvation and announcement of salvation. Not only in its content, however, but also already in its mere existence and its universal approach lies eschatological hope. It is as mediation of hope, hope itself. It is not a doctrine of hope, but the sacrament of hope, that is, future of salvation contained in Word. Similarly, the Lord's Supper is "proclamation of the death of Christ" in its content, but anticipation of the future ("until he comes") in its occurrence. In the Fourth Gospel the paraclete similarly glorifies Christ, but that he glorifies him is a making present of the future. Therefore, the parousia of Christ is seldom "confessed" in confessional formulas of primitive Christian worship, but the Christ confession understands itself as the execution of the parousia hope.[48] The subject matter that is illumined through Easter is the cross. The person who is glorified through Easter is the crucified Christ. The mode, however, in which the future mediated in the crucified one is further mediated is the verbal and spiritual parousia of Christ. This happens in the commissioning of the congregation

---

47. Cf. W. Marxsen, U. Wilckens, G. Delling, H. G. Geyer, *Die Bedeutung der Auferstehungsbotschaft für den Glauben an Jesus Christus* (1966).

48. This has been strongly emphasized by H. Conzelmann, *op. cit.,* pp. 360 f.

with the Word and in its mission into the world of need. St. Paul understands his Gospel as Word-prolepsis of the coming Lord, and himself in his missionary commission as apocalyptic missionary and apostle of the exalted and coming Lord of the world. His mission intends to introduce the obedience of faith in a godless world. It does not intend to promulgate apocalyptic doctrines. The proclamation, however, takes place in order to introduce the obedience of faith within an apocalyptic self-consciousness.

Easter establishes the mission of the believer. Therefore, the great commission which one perceives from the appearances of the risen one precedes the founding of the church chronologically and materially. This implies, conversely, that one cannot have the Easter faith except as in the consciousness of being indebted by it to Jew and Gentile. One can partake of the Gospel only in that one brings it to those for whom it is meant. Church is thus church of the apostolate. And the obedience of faith is participation in the mission of the Gospel into the world. Easter faith establishes a definite concrete initiative and cannot be maintained without it. Christian eschatology is not an apocalyptic explanation of the world and also not a private illumination of existence, but the horizon of expectation for a world transforming initiative through which "the renewal of the world is anticipated in this age in a certain sense."[49] The

---

49. *Dogmatic Constitution on the Church*, art. 48: "*Renovatio mundi in hoc saeculo reali quodam modo anticipatur.*" The phrase "*quodam modo*" can be more precisely defined if one recalls the first *ecclesia* of the Gentiles. Besides the post-Easter constitution of a Jewish-Christian synagogue around "the Twelve," who represent in expectation of the coming Son of Man the messianic renewal of the people of the twelve tribes, there originates out of the circle of "the Seven" (Stephen) in Antioch the *ecclesia* in which Gentiles become disciples without having become proselytes first. The promise that after Israel's redemption the Gentiles will share in it is in the *ecclesia* no longer a mere expectation for God to fulfill, but becomes fulfilled in the word of faith. An eschatological promise has been turned into a present missionary task. It makes the eschatological salvation present outside of Israel, circumventing Israel: the last (the Gentiles) become the first, and the first (the Jews) become the last. What happens to the Gentiles in this anticipation of non-Jewish salvation is a revaluation of the Jewish order of hope

ways in which, through Christian initiative, the transformation of the world is "anticipated" are determined by the real predicament of man, as it is opened up in the anticipation of the judgment of the world in the cross of Christ. Thus one must view together the anticipating initiative and the real predicament of man.

1. The first deed of the eschatological hope is the proclamation of the Gospel of the kingdom to the poor, as it is called in the Gospels, and the proclamation of the righteousness of God to Jews and Gentiles, insofar as all have sinned, as St. Paul puts it. The Gospel addresses itself to all men without "distinction," however, not to all men in the positions of the humanity claimed by them, but to all men in their common lack of true humanity, or their common plight of guilt, suffering, sorrow, and death. In the positive, men separate from one another: Jews from Gentiles, Greeks from barbarians, lords from servants, and so forth. In the negative, however, all stand in a deep and wide solidarity. The Gospel anticipates the future of God at the front of man's real misery in that it offers the lost and the forsaken God's hope.[50]

2. The second deed of hope lies in the founding of the Christian congregation. It constitutes itself not from those

---

corresponding to the resurrection of the crucified one through God. The mission of the *ecclesia* to the nations originates in terms of its self-understanding not from the delay of the parousia and consequent disappointment, but from a reversal of the order of the parousia, and thus from an active anticipation of the world-wide political parousia of Christ. It is not that the concrete eschatology of Jesus (the kingdom of Israel) had turned into the abstract eschatology of "the last things" in the church (against E. Peterson, "Die Kirche," in *Theologische Traktate* [1951], pp. 412 f.). The world-wide mission from which the church of the Jews and Gentiles emerged understood the future of the Gentiles in terms of presence, and the presence of God for Israel as future, and thus arrived at a new concrete eschatology. Cf. E. Käsemann, *op. cit.*, II, pp. 262 f.

50. What this means practically has been made especially clear by W. Stringfellow, *My People Is the Enemy* (1964), and G. Webber, *God's Colony in Man's World* (1960).

who are equal, but from those who differ, for it constitutes itself always at the borderlines where men distinguish themselves from one another through the positive in them in order to assert themselves. Only as the "new people of God" from Jews and Gentiles, Greeks and barbarians, masters and servants, white and black, and so forth, does the congregation stand congruous with that future of God which it proclaims. And only in disregard of such borderlines does it become the sign and sacrament of hope.

3. The third deed of hope is the creative, battling, and loving obedience ready to suffer in the everyday situations of the present world. It is the attempt, under the conditions of estrangement, to live already here out of the promised future of our true home.[51] It is transformation of life, transformation of society, transformation of the world in the possibilities that one is afforded or that one meets, favoring the new life, the new community, the new world. Obedience in the body is anticipation of the redemption of the body (1 Cor. 6),[52] and societal obedience is anticipation of the new humanity which is coming, and earthly obedience is anticipation of the renewal of the earth in the kingdom of God. These anticipations are possible in the discipleship of Jesus who is the reality-prolepsis of God's future. In the context of the Gospel to the poor and of the congregation of the lowly and forsaken (1 Cor. 1, 20 ff.) Christian ethics is the forward-moving, evolutionary and revolutionary initiative for the overcoming of man's bodily predicament and the plight of injustice.

51. H. Schlier, *Besinnung auf das Neue Testament,* II (1954), p. 356: "The admonition implies the expectation that justice be done to the future which has opened itself to him in Christ Jesus and to live from it already in thought and deed."

52. Käsemann, *op. cit.,* II, p. 129: "In that . . . those who belong to him already today deliver that part of the world which they themselves are to Christ in bodily obedience, they testify to his reign as that of the 'cosmocrator' and thus figuratively anticipate the last future of the resurrection reality and of the unlimited *regnum Christi.*"

The eschatological concept of history in which the faith in the reality-prolepsis of God's future in the crucified Christ becomes conscious of itself is no theory of world history and no illumination of the history of existence, but a "battle doctrine" with the cross as victory emblem. This concept does not want to interpret the world religiously, but wants to transform it through creation of the obedience of faith.[53] The Christian view of history does not make the contradictions of the world logical, but places itself in revolutionary contradiction to the present form of the world. It does not, with the eyes of the owl of Minerva, look back upon history completed in order to find the real rational and the rational real,[54] but stands in the dawn of the

---

53. In appropriating Marx's eleventh thesis against Feuerbach (K. Marx, *Frühschriften* [ed. Landshut] [1953], p. 341), I believe I must distinguish my approach from that of hermeneutical and linguistic theology. Language analysis and hermeneutic of traditional ways of talking about God which disregard the function of language in society, politics, and history apparently presuppose that nothing new can and must happen, that society is a closed society and that history has come to an end insofar as the theological task seems to be nothing more than the true interpretation of reality. If this presupposition is proved wrong by reality and the Word, then we must understand reality historically, society as open, and language as political-intentional talk which wants to bring new future into the present conditions in order to change them.

54. G. W. F. Hegel, *Grundlinien der Philosophie des Rechtes* (ed. J. Hoffmeister) (1956), Vorrede, p. 14. Cf. also p. 17: "In order still to say a word about the *instruction* what the world should be like, philosophy arrives at this point always too late anyway. As the *thought* of the world, philosophy appears only in that period after reality has completed its process of cultural formation and has completed itself. . . . If philosophy paints its gray in gray, a form of life has become old, and through gray in gray it cannot be rejuvenated, but merely recognized; the owl of Minerva begins her flight only at the onset of twilight." What distinguishes hermeneutic theology, which wants to set "reality . . . in words" as "a precious stone shows to full advantage only when it is properly cut and set" (G. Ebeling, *God and Word* [1967], p. 23), principally from this kind of approach? Is "reality" already "a precious stone"? Has it already completed its process of cultural formation and become finished? Hegel was able with his philosophy to "capture his time in thoughts" because his reason wanted "to recognize the rose in the cross of the present and herein to enjoy it," and this "reasonable insight" claimed to be "the reconciliation with reality" (*ibid.*, p. 16). And yet neither the cross of his day

coming kingdom and is thus ready to rise up in a world ready to break up. A Christian concept of history is a concept of the reign of Christ in view of the history of the predicament of man and world. One knows that herein the crises of history are not overcome, but that the eschatological crisis of the world becomes manifest. "Where deliverance nears, the danger grows" (Bloch-Hölderlin). Where faith appears, unfaith appears also. Where there is baptism, there is temptation also. Where Christ is present, the anti-Christ comes. Where the future of salvation is anticipated, "the mystery of lawlessness" comes to the fore unconcealed. A Christian understanding of history stands in the service of the historical activity and suffering of the Christians. It lifts eschatological faith, eschatological proclamation, eschatological communion, and eschatological activity into historical self-consciousness.

Demythologizing in Revolutionary and Missionary Interpretation

Ludwig Feuerbach demythologized theology (God is God) via Christology (God became man) as anthropology (man together with man is God).[55] His humanism represented

---

nor the cross of our day, nor the cross of Christ can bring about recognition of the rose and its immediate enjoyment. If by this rose is meant reconciliation through the cross and the reconstitution of the crucified one in the ideality (resurrection) of God, the rose of reconciliation can perhaps be the beginning of the actual transformation of the world which is losing itself in the darkness of the speculative Good Friday. The symbol of theology and philosophy as to transformation on the basis of reconciliation, in this case, would no longer be the owl of the evening, but Minerva herself as goddess of the light of the morning ("The night is far gone, the day is at hand" [Rom. 13, 12].).
Cf. E. Bloch, *Subject-Object, Erläuterungen zu Hegel* (1952); W. D. Marsch, *Gegenwart Christi in der Gesellschaft. Eine Studie zu Hegels Dialektik* (1965).

55. *Das Wesen des Christentums* (1841); *Das Wesen der Religion* (1845).

itself as the consistent fulfillment of the humanization of God through Christianity and the Lutheran Reformation. His critique of the heaven of religion led to the justification of the earth as it is. His "Philosophy of the Future" made man, nature included, the highest object of philosophy, and anthropology, physiology included, the universal science. "Man together with man—the unity of 'I' and 'Thou' is God."[56]

Karl Marx appropriated this criticism of religion, but changed it fundamentally. Criticism of religion for him is not justification of the earth as it is, but basis of every critique of the earth. "The religious misery is at once the expression of the real misery and the protest against the real misery. . . . The critique of religion ends with the doctrine that man is the highest being for man, consequently with the categorical imperative to overturn all conditions in which man is a humiliated, enslaved, forsaken, contemptible being."[57] This critique of religion of the young Marx thus does not demythologize religion as a scientifically antiquated, theistic world view, but wants to put religion on its feet as "protest against the real misery." As transfigured reflection of the real misery, religion is destroyed; as protest against the real misery it is set going in the categorical imperative of revolution.

Of course, one must ask whether Christianity as hope and protest against the real misery of man has been truly

56. L. Feuerbach, *Grundsätze der Philosophie der Zukunft* (1843) (*Kleine philosophische Schriften, PhB,* 227, [1950]), §§ 54, 56, 60, 62.
57. *Frühschriften, op. cit.,* p. 208. One should compare here the corresponding sentence in Feuerbach, *Wesen des Christentums,* p. 201: "This free air of the heart, this articulated secret, this manifest pain of the soul is God. God is a tear of love, shed in deepest hiddenness over the human misery. 'God is an inarticulate sigh in the ground of human souls' (Sebastian Frank von Wörd). This word is the most noteworthy, the deepest, truest expression of Christian mysticism." If with Feuerbach, quite mystically, "God" is a sigh from the ground of the soul, that is, from the ground of existence, with Marx "God" is the expression of the real, that is, the historico-societal ground of human misery. Thus his criticism of religion and his demythologizing does not end with the co-humanity of I and Thou, but with social revolution.

inherited in Marx's theory of revolutionary practice and particularly in the societal practice that calls itself "Marxist." In any case, it is correct, however, that Christian eschatology contains the critique of the estranged heaven as well as of the estranged earth, since it hopes not only for a new earth, but also for a new heaven. For this reason the Christian faith must demythologize and demystify its religious notions. It is also correct that Christian faith hears in the Christ event the categorical imperative for the anticipating transformation of the world of need. For Feuerbach, anthropology became the universal science. For Marx, the revolutionary science of history became the universal science.[58] For overcoming the straits into which demythologizing for the purpose of existential interpretation leads today one can employ Marx's critique of Feuerbach.

1. Underlying the world views of the past is (a) the insight into the real misery of man and world and (b) an initiative for the overcoming of the misery. Criticism of the so-called mythological world views of former theologies remains superficial and caught in the naïve pathos of the Enlightenment if it does not understand these world views as expression of the real misery of man and as protest against it. Myth is not only explanation of the world and expression of human self-understanding, but also expression of the misery of the world and protest against it.

2. An interpretation of the theological projects of the past can, therefore, not use man's self-understanding as the continuum of the receptive and transforming interpretation, but must take the initiative for the transformation of the human predicament (which expresses itself in these projects) as the continuum and reference point of interpretation.[59]

58. *Frühschriften, op. cit.,* p. 346: "We know only one science, the science of history." History has two sides for him: man and nature. Therefore the "history of nature" and the "history of man" condition each other.

59. Against H. Braun, "Die Problematik einer Theologie des Neuen Testaments," *ZThK,* Beiheft 2 (1961), p. 14: "The right co-humanity is

Existential interpretation thus far contains an abstract, unhistorical, and unsocial thinking about man. It informs Christian theology with an unhistorical anthropology and thus ends with Feuerbach.[60] Its separation of subjectivity and objectivity in the notion of objectification, of history and man, and of individual and society leads to the "love-drivel" (Marx) of the co-humanity between "I" and "Thou" in which "God" is supposed to dwell. Because it does not understand the mythological world views as expression of the real misery of man, demythologizing does not arrive at that categorical imperative of the transformation of the world in need. Underlying the New Testament texts, however, is a definite societal initiative, the apostolic service of introducing the obedience and the freedom of faith in a godless and godforsaken world. These are texts of the apostolate or of proclamation. They express the categorical imperative of the resurrected one: through the Gospel, the new communion, and the new obedience, to overturn all conditions in which man is a humiliated, forsaken, and contemptible being, that is, to anticipate at the front of the real misery of man the future of his real being out of God. Our reception of both categories of Marx is thereby merely formal: the real misery of man in the New Testament is seen in his self-inflicted servitude under the powers of sin

---

the multivarious content of the New Testament directives." Cf. "Der Sinn der neutestamentlichen Christologie," *ZThK* (1957), pp. 360 ff.: "The constant is the self-understanding of the faithful, Christology is the variable." R. Bultmann has appropriated the idea. Cf. his *Das Verhältnis der urchristlichen Christusbotschaft zum historischen Jesus* (1960), p. 22. For an opposing perspective see E. Käsemann, "Sackgassen im Streit um den historischen Jesus," in *op. cit.*, II, pp. 31 ff.

60. Compare Feuerbach with H. Braun, *ZThK,* Beiheft 2, p. 18: "Man as man, man in his co-humanity, implies God." See also G. Ebeling, *God and Word* (1967), p. 27: "The meaning of the word God . . . is the basic situation of man as word situation." This is not supposed to be a definition, but a pointer for the use of the word God in language. Should, however, the language of the Gospel speak of God only as the mystery of reality and of the basic situation of man, I do not see that this language could lead beyond the "sign of the ground of the soul."

and death. The categorical imperative which leads to the historical initiative for the overcoming of this misery in correspondence to the justification of the godless is the election of the lowly and the gift of world-conquering hope to the dying. The bodily obedience towards the coming Lord stands in the service of love to the laboring and heavily laden, the humiliated and the insulted.

Also, the form-critical view of the New Testament texts, as the sociological view that it is, discovers the front of the missionized and missionary groups in the world. The content and form of their language thus cannot be understood apart from a consideration of their initiative over against the real misery of men in their time. The constant in the various messages of the New Testament is, therefore, not anthropology (H. Braun), but the societal initiative, that is, mission. Since this initiative unites the hope for the wretched with the name and the history of Jesus, the reference to Jesus is constant and constitutive in the multiple forms of this initiative towards Jews and Gentiles.

A modern hermeneutic which takes this into consideration will understand the New Testament and interpret it apostolically as manual of the Christian mission. It will not only ask how these texts must be understood and how they must be proclaimed today, but it will ask antecedently what necessitated these texts, in order to indicate why they must be preached today. The New Testament testimonies have one intention and one tendency: they originate in the movements of the apostolate and they point to the movement of the apostolate "until he comes." The goal of the interpretation must, therefore, correspond to the goal of the texts themselves. The goal of Christ's history which is here told and proclaimed is the political parousia of Christ in universal glory. In that the words proclaim Christ, they announce his universal future. Hermeneutic stands in the missionary context, and in the interpretation of the Christ event it must develop the universal horizon of the future. In its interpretation of the Christ event, it must develop for present-day experience in its predicament the universal future of Christ. Hermeneutic today must thus serve the apostolic initiative. The variableness of the interpretation is governed by the historically changing forms of the real misery of man. Constant is the origin of the interpretation in the resurrection of the crucified one. Constant is the tendency of the interpretation which aims for the overcoming of the real misery of man in the coming of the kingdom. The understanding that spans the various historical periods is made possible on account of the solidarity of the wretched and their contemporaneousness relative to the new future of salvation in Christ opened up for them.

Creative Eschatology[61]

How does the mission of the Christians for the future of the world realize itself? It cannot be realized in contemplation, since contemplation relates to that which has come into existence or to the eternally existing. The future of the world that Christians hope for, however, is in its reality something still expected and thus also something still originating and coming. The Christian hope in the Spirit anticipates this future and brings it into the present. This means that the Christian hope must be creative and militant. For the Christian hope, the eschaton, the kingdom, and the city of God do not simply lie in readiness like the future of the new aeon in apocalypticism, so that one could only relate to it in conceptualization and wait for it by leaving the present as it is.

In that the future is anticipated in hope, it is in the process of coming. We are construction workers and not only interpreters of the future whose power in hope as well as in fulfillment is God (Metz). The Christians must under-

---

61. I am here appropriating ideas expressed by J. B. Metz in his Chicago lecture in April 1966. Cf. *Orientierung,* 30:9 (May 15, 1966), pp. 107–109.

stand themselves as "co-workers" of the promised kingdom of God and its universal peace and its righteousness. For they live not for a future which has not begun as yet, but which has already arrived in Christ and which—coming from him—will change the world. If the Christians hope for this future of God, they not only wait for it, but also look for it, love it, and strive for it. The eschatological will leads to decisions that are live options in the present. The decision for the goal determines the means and ways that lead to the goal.[62] In the living correspondence of the Christians to this future, the future already finds a real form. Christian eschatology is, therefore, not only receptive but also productive, not only passive but also militant hope for the future. It directs itself upon the *one* future of everything we comprehend in history. For the future is the one and only future because it is God's future. It is the future of the whole, since it is the future of salvation. Consequently, there are no longer several futures, but the one future of God and salvation will be gained or impeded at all the intellectual and physical, individual and social fronts of the present predicament. Only this eschatological horizon of the hope for the one future of the world from the one God is wide enough in order to confront faith with the present needs and necessities and to introduce it into life.

An eschatology of the world that is necessitated hereby in order to get the creative and militant hope of the Christians on the road of living obedience can therefore no longer be developed in the style and with the categories of the old theological cosmology. If the real predicament underlying the theistic world view was the theodicy question (*Si Deus,*

---

62. St. Thomas in keeping with Aristotle: The choosing ($προαίρεσις$) directs itself not upon the impossible . . . , the willing ($βούλησις$), however, directs itself (also) upon the impossible as, for example, immortality. Choosing pertains to those things over which we can exercise power. But willing can go beyond that. In willing and intending lies a decision for the goal itself. In the choosing lie the decisions about the ways and means that lead towards the goal.

unde malum?), the Christian initiative for the overcoming of this predicament today, using the possibilities of the modern world, must enter the battle for God's righteousness on earth politically in the battle against human misery. Therefore, cosmological theology must now be replaced by *political theology*. In political theology the future of God is mediated in the world changing powers of man, so that today this future makes these powers and possibilities of man legitimate in their use and they anticipate it at the front of the present misery. Now the *malum,* to the extent that it was created by man, no longer turns against God, but God turns against the *malum.* The question: if God is, why is there still evil in the world? becomes an accusation not against God, but against ourselves, and is answered, to begin with, through the *verum facere* of the Christians in their various vocations directed to the world of misery.

This eschatology of the world which as political theology replaces the old theological cosmology, furthermore, takes the theology of existence and of personal faith into itself. If underlying these theologies of personal existence-illumination is the question of identity, this question finds its concrete answer through the identification of the believer with his calling to be a co-worker of the kingdom of God. The way in which in the world of non-identity, fragmentation, and darkness as regards himself man is given identity is the way of conscious and hoping renunciation. In the world of sin and death Christ has realized his identity with God (Phil. 2) and has thus conquered the power of alienation. Only in the correspondence to his self-realization through self-renunciation will the believers find themselves and their true being: only he who loses himself—for the sake of Christ and the Gospel of the kingdom—will find himself, in eternal life which is the future of God. The way in which the power of self-estrangement is here broken is the way of self-renunciation in favor of a human and free world of God that is our home. Thus the Christian answer to the fundamental identity question of man leads man to the practical answering of the theodicy question. Political theology unites cosmological theology and the theology of existence in the eschatological understanding of the history of man and world.

Finally, we must, however, consider once more that it would be impossible to anticipate the future if the future were not coming towards us. The real future is not identical with the successes of our activity. It must come towards us in order that our activity be "not in vain" (1 Cor. 15, 58). All militant efforts to introduce a better future are blind in this respect, for they think of man as good while evil supposedly only dwells in the conditions that must be overcome or in the enemies that must be conquered. They do not see that man himself is an ambivalent being and that he, since the evil is lodged also in himself, is destroyer as well as builder of the future. "Did the Ironsides bring brotherhood, the Jacobines freedom, the Bolsheviks equality?"[63] Obviously, always something different resulted from what one actually wanted. For "hidden in the *citoyen* of the French Revolution was the *bourgeois*. God have mercy on us as to what hides in the comrade!"[64] The English Revolution did not bring the kingdom of God but democracy. The Industrial Revolution did not bring the kingdom of reason but the irrationality of civilization dynamics. The Russian Revolution did not bring the classless society but a bureaucratic system of functionaries and specialists. Thus revolution, where it establishes itself, swallows its own hopes in order to cover up the shame of its "accomplishments." It eats up its fathers and orphans its children. The deeper problem of this ambiguity of action lies in the fact that it is logically and practically impossible to anticipate the end of history under the conditions of history, that it is impos-

63. C. Fr. von Weizsäcker, *Die Tragweite der Wissenschaft,* I (1964), p. 185.
64. E. Bloch, *Spuren* (1959), p. 30. See also *ibid.*, p. 32: "But what hides in the comrade, really hides in him, and not in the circumstances which make men still more queer. . . . man is something which still must be found."

sible under the conditions of estrangement and as one who himself is estranged to anticipate the home of true humanity, that it is impossible as a sinner to overcome sin.[65] Thus out of this battle always new history emerges, new estrangement of man and new sin. In order to be able to act with certainty in the face of this impossibility, we need the consciousness that this future is not built with our own hands but comes towards us with forbearance. Bertolt Brecht in exile expressed this insight in the battle against Hitler's Reich:

> We who wished to prepare the soil for kindness
> could not be kind ourselves.
> But you, when at last it will come to pass that man
> is a helper to man,
> remember us with forbearance.

Only the consciousness to be dependent on the forbearance of the coming ones or the coming-towards-us of the future can bring unity into the difference, and unequivocalness into the equivocalness of the present activity for the future. If the future does not bring redemption from the

---

65. Löwith (*Gesammelte Abhandlungen zur Kritik der christlichen Überlieferung* [1966], p. 133) has called this *"the* difference in the philosophy of history," to which already the double meaning of *pragmata* as event and act points. "History tells of events which have been evoked by the acts of man. *But the events are never congruous with the acts.* Without the difference it would remain inexplicable why in history always something totally different results than was intended by the actors." *Bossuet* discovered herein the confluence of human thought and divine direction; *Vico* the ground for the fact that human intentions always stand in the service of another ultimate purpose; *Kant* the effect of an anonymous "intention of nature" upon free human activity; *Hegel* the "cunning of reason" which uses great men as agents of the world spirit; and, finally, *Marx* the circumstance that economic and social being determines consciousness. *Freud* made the power of the unconscious responsible for this difference in the philosophy of history. Basically, however, the difference in the historical activity of men between intention and success, departure and arrival, originates in the ambivalent constitution of man himself, who discovers himself in the ontological difference between existence and essence, being-there and Being, and who must move therein.

conditions under which it is here prepared as well as impeded, the future cannot be gained. The "realm of freedom" can thus not be the result of the "realm of work and necessity." It then remains an infinite goal and an unattainable bonus of our ambivalent activity. The "realm of freedom," by definition, and also in the present consciousness, must show the characteristic of coming freely (*gratis data*).[66] The future can thus not be thought of as the infinite and unattainable goal of acting and seeking here, but must be believed in as the coming redemption from coercions and necessities under which we must act in the present. The kingdom of God can only then be understood as the real future of the world if it becomes present in history as redemption and as goal of the human striving, as absolution in forgiveness of sins and as goal of new obedience. The surplus value of the future above and beyond the attained and the attainable shows itself not only in permanent surplus of incentive, but always also as redemption from the compulsions of the instincts. Only in this doubleness of anticipation and already arrived grace (*Zuvorkommenheit*), of redemption and mobilization, does the future work into the misery of the present in a humanizing way. It is exactly this double impression of the future upon history which we discover in the resurrection of the crucified one and in the cross of the risen Christ.

66. Also in *Marx* the significance of work for the "realm of freedom" is ambivalent. On the one hand, the realm of freedom is identical with the elimination of work and necessity: work changes into pure spontaneity and play. On the other hand, the realm of freedom results from the realm of the necessity of work: the more and more rationally organized work introduces unburdening opportunities for freedom. On the one hand, the realm of freedom comes in a "leap" and in sudden change from quantity to quality. But this is only a different word for "miracle." On the other hand, the space for freedom is created through making work more rational. The first would be a community of free individuals not estranged: total man. The second, however, would be merely a leisure time society of playboys who are not known to be very thoughtful people in the first place.

TOWARDS THE WAITING GOD

Frederick Herzog

It has occasionally been suggested in recent theological discourse that only now in the history of the church is the question of hope moving into the center of theological reflection. Reference is being made to Kant's dictum: "The whole interest of reason, speculative as well as practical, is centered in the three following questions: (1) What can I know? (2) What ought I to do? (3) What may I hope?"[1] Carl E. Braaten comments that modern theology since Kant has concerned itself with the first question and to some extent with the second, but hardly with the third, "the question of hope, the self-transcending movement of man towards his future."[2] This may appear strange, since one can regard the Enlightenment as the beginning of the Age of Hope in Western civilization. Is theology only now becoming fully conscious of its responsibility for the innermost aspirations of modernity? This can hardly be said. What is now happening is that some theologies are trying to reinterpret biblical eschatology in such a way that its message of hope can be understood by modern man.[3]

1. *Critique of Pure Reason* (London, 1934), p. 457.
2. "Toward a Theology of Hope," *Theology Today,* 24:2 (July 1967), p. 208.
3. For a discussion of recent reinterpretation of biblical eschatology see Jürgen Moltmann, "Probleme der neueren evangelischen Eschatologie," *Verkündigung und Forschung,* 11:2 (1966), pp. 100–124.

This in my view is the prime significance of Jürgen Moltmann's *Theology of Hope*. It merges the great modern yearning for the transformation of the world with the eschatological message of the Bible. It seeks to energize the hope of modernity. But it also offers a critical vantage point. Too long has the hope of modernity been isolated from faith. And too long has faith neglected the needs of modern hope.

Beyond This Darkness

The theology of hope has its Sitz im Leben *in the almost desperate reluctance of our age to give up the future.*

The hope of modern man often seemed to be hidden behind a dark cloud. But it always disappeared only for a while, all the more forcefully to appear again. For example, the agony and the travail of the Second World War became a new impetus for a reappearance of hope. One of the first theologies of hope to appear after the war was Roger Shinn's *Beyond This Darkness*. In the preface he suggests: "Christianity offers a hope that is real, but no one has a right to talk of that hope unless he has looked hard at the stark facts of our time."[4] Speaking of his own experience, of having had to face "torn and burning flesh, painful masses of blood and mangled muscles," he was reminded of what Ernie Pyle had called an "almost desperate reluctance to give up the future."[5] Man hopes somehow to be able to claim the future for life. Facing the hydrogen bomb and the Vietnam War, mankind today is questing for a time when these threats will have ceased. The question has remained the same, whether raised at the end of the Second World War or now in the midst of the Vietnam War. Said Shinn shortly after the Second World War: "The question is whether we can find any meaning in the confusion and

4. (New York, 1946) p. vii.
5. *Ibid.*, pp. 19 f.

conflict of things—whether God is here. The question keeps coming back to us in various ways. It concerns those who have suffered from the cruelties of an age of furious hates and calculated destruction. Again it meets those who have been driven by the impersonal forces of our time to inflict suffering for the sake of something better. Finally, it centers in each of us who looks with fear into a world and a history which he does not understand. Yet the question is always the same. It is the search for hope in the midst of uncertainty and fear."[6]

Since the publication of Shinn's little volume this search has developed into a distinct movement of theological thought, first fully articulated in European theology. In America interest in it is beginning to gain momentum. Not everyone will think *The New York Times*' recent headline felicitous: " 'God is Dead' Doctrine Is Losing Ground to the 'Theology of Hope'."[7] But the interest in a new movement is unmistakable. It became Jürgen Moltmann's fate that in the title of his book he coined a phrase that distinctly characterized the movement as the theology of hope.[8]

It is understood that it is a theology of hope not in the midst of a new optimism, although there is also some of that around,[9] but in the face of much absurdity. The signs of the times are not principally hopeful. In a student symposium held at Duke University on "The Post-War Generation," Jack Newfield spoke of the prophetic vision of this generation as that of comic-apocalyptic absurdity and chaos: "Logic, rules, and dogmas explain less and less about a society that puts Martin King and Joan Baez in jail, and Lurleen Wallace and Ronald Reagan in power. . . . Or a

---

6. *Ibid.*, p. 85.
7. (March 24, 1968) p. 1.
8. Some (foremost Vernard Eller) have insisted that "theology of hope" is a misnomer, that one should rather speak of a theology of promise. See, for example, his "Comments on an Unsolicited Series," *The Christian Century*, 85:15 (April 10, 1968), pp. 459 f.
9. Cf. William Hamilton, "The New Optimism—From Prufrock to Ringo," *Theology Today*, 22:4 (January 1966), pp. 479–490.

society that sends 525,000 troops to Asia, but not 82 voting registrars to Mississippi."[10] *The Christian Century,* in its annual "shape of the year editorial," December 27, 1967, echoed this feeling of absurdity and spoke of the present sickness of America as a sickness unto death. But it also spoke of hope: "We have occasion now to learn something about the context of Christian hope. It is 'crucified' hope, born in spite of Babel and at Golgotha, in the midst of a world sick unto death. It depends not on journalistic optimism or sociological documentation, but on the promise of God. It is 'resurrected' hope, born in the midst of a world that shows few signs of resurrection, gives no evidence that the new creation has begun, and is always on the verge of happening to us."[11]

During 1967 *The Christian Century* had brought an unsolicited series of articles on hope.[12] By and large, all spoke of the tension between the absurdity of our age, on the one hand, and the strong longing to overcome it, on the other. But they also revealed at least two tendencies of approaching the matter of hope that are somewhat distinct, the one holding a more philosophical and the other a more biblical perspective.

In the last article of the series, "What Hope For Hope?",[13] Leon J. Putnam gives a more philosophical analysis of hope and distinguishes it from optimism, which he regards as the notion that change will somehow bring a better day. Hope he views as realistic confidence in what one can expect of the future. It involves the willingness to face the risk of failure. But it also creates community: "Hope fires hope." Hope completely interiorized would not be hope. It is always also concerned about the future of others. Basically, it belongs to the very structure of man's being. This seems in accord with Gabriel Marcel, who declared that "hope is perhaps the very stuff of which our soul is made."

10. *The Duke Chronicle,* 63:25 (November 6, 1967), p. 2.
11. 84:52, p. 1645.
12. Beginning with its November 1, 1967, issue.
13. 84:48 (November 29, 1967), pp. 1519–1521.

Putnam ends with a criticism of the more biblically oriented view of Harvey Cox, who wishes to speak of God as the one who *will be* rather than the one who *is*. Putnam argues more for hope on grounds of an eternal here and now and a present presence of the past. Here we have, in the midst of the American discussion about hope, the major formal aspect of the central problem of present-day Protestant theology: whether we wish to stress a more philosophical or a more biblical view of God. The biblical view confronts us with God in history. The philosophical approach demands a more ontological perspective. It should be understood that the issue is now not one of emphasizing the biblical view to the exclusion of the philosophical or the philosophical to the exclusion of the biblical. It is a matter of which one becomes the heuristic principle of theological thought.[14] As to the future of theology, it will make a big difference which principle wins out. More biblically oriented theologians of hope have again forcefully introduced the theodicy question of the Bible: When will God be fully God? When will he be justified in his ways with man? Present philosophical discussion about hope may not even be bothered by this question.

The God of Hope

From the triad of theological virtues—faith, hope, and love—the theology of hope selects hope as the most viable response to God in our age.

For the *American* scene, the initial significance of the theology of hope lies in its contribution to the question of God. Whether one turns to John Macquarrie's recent book *God and Secularity*[15] or to Carl F. H. Henry's recent article in *Christianity Today* on "Where Is Modern Theology

---

14. Cf. my "God, Evil and Revolution," *The Journal of Religious Thought,* 25:2 (Autumn-Winter 1968–69), p. 8.
15. (Philadelphia, 1967.)

Going?",[16] the principal opinion expressed over a wide range of theological positions is the same: the God question is the focus of the present theological debate. The reasons for the emergence of this question are too numerous to mention. For example, we wonder how we can still believe in God in a world more and more controlled by man. Or we ask, why should we believe in God in the face of the evils of our age?

It would be inaccurate to say that the theology of hope focuses on the God question. It focuses on hope. But in so doing it cannot avoid turning to *the ground of hope*. And before long the theology of hope becomes a wrestle with the "God of hope." This means that the theology of hope directs us also to a reëxamination of the biblical view of God.

Part of the new perspective can be explained by the way the concern for hope began to take shape in European Protestant theology. Since the development of dialectical theology in the early twenties, a theology of the Word had dominated Protestant Europe, whether in terms of Barth's *Church Dogmatics* or Bultmann's kerygma theology. From here, European Protestant theology found its strong orientation in biblical thought. In Moltmann's *Theology of Hope* we are once more confronted with the major thrust of this concern. But while dialectical theology developed into a theology of faith in response to the grace of the Word, Moltmann moved into a theology of hope grounded in the promise of the Word.

By the beginning of the sixties, the Pannenberg circle had begun to question the adequacy of the theology of the Word as developed by Barth and Bultmann. As this group of young theologians saw it, the Word had been too rigidly understood as focus of God's self-communication.[17] They generally argued that neither the Old nor New Testament

---

16. 92:11 (March 1, 1968), pp. 3 f.
17. See Wolfhart Pannenberg (ed.), *Offenbarung als Geschichte* (Göttingen, 1961).

speaks uniformly of the Word of God as the place of God's self-communication. The name of God and his law are as little places of God's self-communication as his Word. God is not communicated through words as such at all, but through his historical acts in conjunction with his words. Only the totality of God's acting and speaking shows, in an *indirect* way, who God is.

An indirect communication, for Pannenberg, initially at least, differs from what is to be communicated. In a direct communication that which is to be communicated moves directly from the communicator to the receiver. In indirect communication God is not the immediate subject matter. So each historical act of God only partially reflects the reality of God. There are always other acts that complement a particular event. Only the totality of acts can function as revelation of God. Consequently, revelation did not take place in the beginning of God's history with man. It occurs at the end. The indirectness of God's revelation in history points to the cumulative aspect of all of history.

In Jesus Christ we have a prolepsis of the end of all history. In him the truth of all history lies open for everyone to see. If he is encountered in the context of the history in which he appeared, the events of his life will speak their own language, the language of facts. Nothing has to be added to these events in order to make them meaningful. They communicate their own meaning. Men must come to their right senses in order to appreciate the significance of these events. First comes *knowledge* of these events. Only *then* comes faith. And faith is directed towards the future. Faith trusts that God has been revealed in the events of Jesus' life, especially in his resurrection.

In my opinion, the contribution of Pannenberg to the debate about revelation lies in the rejection of the idea of the *principally* hidden God. Pannenberg no longer understands God as primally concealed in some secret hideaway of reality. What keeps man from recognizing God is not a particular idiosyncrasy in the nature of God that would always keep him hidden, but man's inability to view God from the vantage point of the consummation of history.

The progress made by Pannenberg, however, did not come to full fruition in his exclusive concentration on history. The difficulties he seemed to be creating were soon pointed out by men like Moltmann who were taking note of the issues raised in a theology that understood theology as history. First of all, Pannenberg had bracketed out faith from the initial appropriation of God's revelation in Jesus Christ, or so it seemed, since faith was supposed to deal primarily with the future. But was the future really the focus of faith? Was this not the place to speak of hope? Here Moltmann began his critique.

There was the even more pressing difficulty of the emphasis on God's indirect self-communication subject to eschatological consummation. At this point, Moltmann pressed his critique further: "This eschatology acquires its eschatological character only from the fact that reality cannot yet be contemplated as a whole because it has not yet come to an end."[18] As regards revelation, this would ultimately require that the world "will one day be theophany, indirect self-revelation of God *in toto*."

In his critique, Moltmann turned primarily to the concept of history employed by Pannenberg: "This theology of history as opposed to the theology of the word remains subject to Kant's critique of theological metaphysics, as long as it itself fails to undertake critical reflection on the conditions of the possibility of perceiving reality as history in the eschatological and theological sense." As illustration of the uncritical view of the historical, Moltmann pointed to Pannenberg's concept of resurrection: "The thesis that this event of the raising of Jesus must be 'historically' verifiable in principle, would require us first of all to alter the concept of the historical that it would allow of God's raising the dead and would make it possible to see in this raising of the dead the prophesied end of history."

18. *The Theology of Hope* (New York, 1967), p. 79. The following quotations are taken from pp. 79 ff.

Moltmann, in this context, introduced a further modification of the concept of revelation. He, like Pannenberg, stressed the significance of the resurrection, but now in terms of the identity of the risen one with the crucified one. A future element is still involved: "Jesus is recognized in the Easter appearances as what he really *will* be." But the focus is on the future of *Jesus*. Here lies the matrix of Moltmann's understanding of revelation as promise. While it has an eschatological dimension, it is not identified with "an eschatologically oriented view of reality as universal history." Promise points beyond history. It "announces the coming of a not yet existing reality from the future of truth." But the promise is grounded in the identity of cross and resurrection, which depends ultimately on the faithfulness of God. The identity of the risen one with the crucified one "forms the ground of the promise of the still outstanding future of Jesus Christ." Moltmann, too, frees the concept of revelation from the tension between a principally hidden and a manifest God. Only that for him revelation is not in history as such but in the word of promise that first of all creates history. Undoubtedly, there is also an element of the hiddenness of God still operative in Moltmann's thought.[19] But it is not as though for him behind the word of promise there were a reality playing hide-and-seek with man.

In my opinion, we must retain the findings of Moltmann, but press further on their basis. The God of hope reaches from the future time and again into the present and creates history through the word of promise. If this is so, is there still any point to retaining the concept "revelation"?

In terms of a cosmological view of the relationship between God and world, it is understandable that God can be viewed as somehow hidden behind the surface of the visible world. In the existentialist approach of theology to this relationship one can see how God must still remain the hidden mysterious ground of man's self and of all

---

19. Cf. especially *ibid.*, p. 87. The issue needs to be explored much further than we are able to here.

things. But as soon as one approaches God from a radically historical view the perspective changes. In the eschatological emphasis, God appears on the frontier of life in its openness to the future. The whole struggle of atheism at its core seems little more than a rejection of a God who, by theological fiat, is hidden in an obscure or distant recess of reality and does not offer free access to himself for all men.

The emphasis on the word of promise takes revelation out of the realm of the mythological and metaphysical and places it fully in the historical dimension. Does it place revelation, however, radically enough in the dimension of history? In the New Testament it seems that God's history with man compels men to view him as principally open to his creation. He appears in his word of promise that creates history. But does not his Word-presence in history negate the whole problem of revelation as we have been discussing it under Kantian auspices? Does not God's Word-presence, the presence of his transcendence in history, overcome the split between noumena and phenomena, freedom and causality? Perhaps the modern problem of revelation ceases to be a problem once we have grasped the unconcealment in which God is coming towards us in Jesus Christ. Perhaps God is not our problem. It may be that we are our problem. The issue before us then would not be the *deus absconditus,* but the *homo absconditus,* not the hidden God, but hidden man, man hidden to himself. What this involves we can only say after we have more fully considered the significance of Jesus Christ. Before we come to this point, however, we must take care of a few methodological questions that grow out of the previous argument.

As I see it, we cannot begin theology merely from the perspective of hope, on the one hand, and Jesus' death and resurrection, on the other. His *life* as well as his death and resurrection have to be taken into account. We must begin with the life as seen in the light of death and resurrection, so that the entirety of the Christ-event comes into view.

Here is the place to ask whether it is adequate to the

theological subject matter to try to understand theology as eschatology as Jürgen Moltmann wishes to do. The program fits well into the framework of modern reinterpretations of theology, such as theology as *anthropology* (Feuerbach) or theology as *Christology* (Barth). Theology as *eschatology* certainly does not mean theology at the exclusion of theology as Christology. And eschatology for Moltmann hardly becomes the one and only criterion according to which the theological enterprise must be shaped and judged. While he views Christology on the foil of eschatology, he also considers eschatology in the light of Christology. But in the process of developing an eschatological Christology and a Christological eschatology, Jesus Christ seems to appear more as a dogmatic datum than the "live," still point that he is in God's Word-presence. T. S. Eliot says in the *Four Quartets:* "Except for the point, the still point, there would be no dance, and there is only the dance."[20] There is a point where all of theology comes alive. This is the person of Jesus Christ as he appears in God's Word-presence as the living witness of God. It is also a task of theology to recover this point.

Under the influence of the concept of theology as eschatology, Moltmann's view of Jesus Christ centers in two ideas: the anticipation of the future and the incarnation of the future. Christology here concentrates heavily on the work of Christ. But this work does not light up enough in terms of the *worker*. In turning to the richness of Jesus' activity, perhaps other aspects of the reality of God would also come to the fore, not merely God as the God of hope.

The "God of Hope" is a significant emphasis of the New Testament message, an emphasis especially important in our future-oriented age. But if isolated as guiding principle of theological thought, can it fully say what it is supposed to say? We must think of greater complementarity here.

Moltmann likes to appeal to Rev. 1, 4, where God is

20. (London, 1959) pp. 15 f.

spoken of as the one "who is and who was and who is to come." One would expect to read "and who will be." But the chain of being is broken by the biblical God. Thus Moltmann speaks of the God of hope as the "coming God." Our modern experience, however, compels us to ask: *who is coming?* In Samuel Beckett's *Waiting for Godot,* a little boy has a message for two lingering bums: "Mr. Godot told me to tell you he won't come this evening but surely tomorrow."[21] The tomorrow of Godot's coming never comes. There can be an empty, meaningless coming of the future. The crucial matter is how God's coming is qualified, what it is that God is doing in his coming. So I would like to speak of the "coming" God as the waiting God. God's coming implies a waiting, and his waiting a coming. The coming of the future must provide for a new reality experience. Otherwise, nothing might be happening at all.

The Waiting God

Also today theology's primary concern cannot be man's response, but the reality that evokes the response. The primal Sitz im Leben *of theology is the dynamic in front of us that draws us out of ourselves and works at overcoming the plight of the world.*

I wish to think of theology as *theo*logy with two foci, Christology and eschatology. From this perspective, faith appears primarily as response to the offense of the cross, hope as confidence in the future evoked by the resurrection, and love as the power that breaks forth from Jesus' life through cross and resurrection creating faith and hope. Thus the theology of hope might be grounded in a theology of God's waiting, a theology of a strange form of love.

21. (New York, 1954) p. 33.

(A) *The Ground of Hope*

As to the ground of hope, the New Testament speaks of "Christ Jesus our hope" (1 Tim. 1, 1). He proclaims the coming kingdom of God. And he acts in terms of its nearness. So we turn to him in order to understand the origin of our hope. Günther Bornkamm has said: "The same church that expects the coming one and that is certain of his presence in the Spirit commits itself consciously to the way and message of the earthly Jesus and accepts his directive and promise for its own way on earth, not in spite of its future-directed hope, but because of it. Its expectation of the coming one finds its power and its ground in the knowledge of the Then and Now."[22]

What we can learn from the theology of hope is that it was God's *future* in the Then and that it is this *future* in the Now that sustains us. Nevertheless, there was a *Then* of God's nearness in Jesus Christ. Bornkamm stresses how Jesus' countrymen in his day were either captivated by traditions of the past or fascinated by the future without having any real sense of the present. He finds no parallel in Judaism to the immediacy of God's nearness in Jesus. While the Hebrews had a notion of a loving and forgiving God, only now in Jesus' word and deed did God's love become an historical event. And while God's reign over all men was still in the future, in Jesus Christ it was already beginning: "But if it is by the finger of God that I cast out demons, then the kingdom of God has come upon you" (Lk. 11, 20).

Christian hope is thus grounded in what is happening in the merging of future and present in the words and deeds of Jesus Christ. Here I find that some restructuring of Moltmann's order of priorities is called for. In the preceding essay he says: "Faith has the *prius,* since it is the first thing that corresponds in us to God's future. But hope owns the

22. *Jesus von Nazareth* (Stuttgart, 1956), p. 172.

primacy, since in faith everything is directed to God's future and faith owes itself to the opening up of this future. In faith hope finds its ground in Christ's cross. In hope faith finds its end in Christ's parousia. What is grounded on faith and becomes effective through hope is love."[23] Taking note of the earthly Jesus besides his cross and parousia, must we not say that love owns the primacy? Faith and hope are human responses. But God's love in Christ Jesus is their ground. It is this love that generates faith and hope. Thus St. Paul could say that it is love that "believes all things, hopes all things" (1 Cor. 13, 7). That is, love stands here for the unceasing process between future and present that continually binds them together in interaction and that through the word of promise creates history. Only through this history-creating power can we have faith and hope.

(B) *Stumbling-Block and Folly*

One need only read the New Testament superficially to realize immediately that faith and hope do not come easy. Jesus was a puzzlement to all who met him. It was experienced in various ways, too numerous to mention. We are all familiar with them. As the Gospels show over and over again, it happens that men close themselves to what Jesus Christ represents. The response to Jesus in his time reflects man's usual response to God.

The response to Jesus shows that our problem with God is principally not at all one of right spacing or right timing: a shifting from the "God above us" to the "God in us" or from both to the "God ahead of us." It is not a matter of quantification, but of finding a new quality beyond ourselves. Moltmann, too, wants to speak of a new quality. But I do not find him arguing this through as the basic component of a new experience of God, so that the impres-

23. See above, p. 34.

sion of a shift in quantification is given rather than a turn to a new quality of experience. Obviously, because of our more historical frame of mind, we today can better experience God in terms of history and the future. But that is not our basic problem. Our real difficulty is that we cannot find the "Other" that compels us to worship. It is useless to shift around on the spatial and chronological scales of our mind unless we face the question of the otherness of God.[24]

(C) *The Unexpected*

Now, some might exclaim: "Not Karl Barth and Soren Kierkegaard all over again! Not again that line about the infinitely qualitative difference between God and man!" My reply would have to be: Perhaps we have not examined carefully enough the quality of the God experience. We have too often understood the otherness of God as pure transcendence. If we focus on the earthly Jesus, we do find otherness, but not pure transcendence. We find incomparable *sovereignty* in a man: "The crowds were astonished at his teaching, for he taught them as one who had authority, and not as their scribes" (Mt. 7, 29). People were caught unawares, by surprise. Their mouths were stopped.

Something unexpected or unforeseen struck them in Jesus' word and deed. It was a completely new event in their lives. In their cheapskate world they were suddenly confronted with something costly. They were overcome with awe. It was so different from what they had been

---

24. T. S. Eliot in *Four Quartets* plays beautifully on the chronological scale when he says:
"Time present and time past
Are both perhaps present in time future,
And time future contained in time past."
But this moving back and forth on the chronological scale does not really get at man's basic problem with God. I am calling attention to the utterance of a "non-professional" theologian to make it clear that the problem is seen otherwise and is not merely a technical point of theology.

used to. Here was otherness, a new lease on life, new being. Whenever men try to make life safe in their conventions it usually becomes a prison of their feelings and their thoughts. In Jesus something new broke through that denied the conventions their finality.

An analogy may be found in the figure of the fool. Says Enid Welsford: "Whenever the clown baffles the policeman, whenever the fool makes the sage look silly . . . there is a sudden sense of pressure relieved, of a birth of new joy and freedom."[25] Something similar happens in Jesus Christ. Only that in him the unexpected of a dimension breaks through that lies beyond man's power of control: a new world in which man finds his master and thus his freedom. It is not pure transcendence. It is the transcendence of the otherness of a new word in history. It is transcendence *in history,* in the Word-presence of the otherness.

(D) *God Waits on Man*

What in Jesus Christ breaks through our conventions is not merely the startling entrance of a new world, but a supportive power that enables us *to become free.* We have already referred to it as the love of God. But the phrase has become trite. It does not convey the quality of foolishness that suddenly lights into man's puzzlement about life and transforms his conventions. Perhaps we can think of this *foolish coming* of a new lease on life as *God's waiting on man.* Being waited on in Jesus Christ as witness of God seems foolish, since one does not expect to be waited on by ultimate reality. The newness of the experience makes one hold one's breath. It also turns out to be a waiting on man from the future, a waiting that man choose his freedom, arise, and go towards his true home of identity. It is the waiting of the Father in the parable of the Prodigal Son.

Moltmann, in the leading contribution to this book,

---

25. *The Fool: His Social and Literary History* (New York, 1961), pp. 322 f. Cf. my *Understanding God* (New York, 1966), p. 108.

speaks of the "love of God hoping for the future of man."[26] Here he comes close to what I wish to suggest by speaking of God's waiting on man. I would only like to see it articulated as the *lynchpin* of a theology of God's Word-presence, albeit in Moltmann's instance the Word-presence of God's future.

Under the image of this foolish "waiting on," God might again appear to us as the "Other," the enabler of new life, a life we did not expect. The enabling action that reaches, as it were, from the future into the present and holds future and present together is God's waiting on his whole creation. It is persevering creativity, a compelling sovereignty that makes man worship: "My Lord and my God!" (Jn. 20, 28). Waiting in this respect is nothing passive, but the most dynamic activity that man can experience. In my view, this is what man is longing for even today. It is not found in simply turning to our everyday world. We hear time and again that our world has grown almost too large for love. In the New Testament we read of a time when "most men's love will grow cold" (Mt. 24, 12). If we are living in such a time, we need all the more to be confronted with the otherness of God's waiting. We need a new event that can transform our concealment from God.

The center of God's waiting is the cross in which he shares in man's suffering and thereby addresses himself to the *theodicy* question. God does not answer it theoretically. In his waiting on man in the cross he himself knows man's plight.

(E) *Understanding God's Waiting*

What lights into man as the new, lights up the old in man, so that he suddenly realizes that he has concealed himself from the new all along. In Jesus Christ God's principal unconcealment becomes the judgment on man who hides himself from himself. All he needs to do in view of God's

26. See above, p. 33.

unconcealment is to step into the full openness of life and see himself as he really is: the creature that is truly free when he has found his master.

Whenever a man finds a new lease on life, he shows that he has a pre-awareness of God's activity in Jesus Christ. For example, in revolutionary change that contributes to the humanizing of man (of which we speak so much today) we can see a pre-awareness that forestalls God's waiting in Jesus Christ. Man who responds to God's unconcealment, even though he does not understand what is going on, is compelled to transform his experience into ever new transformations of his environment. But only through faith in Jesus Christ can he really understand the inroad of the new.

God's waiting, however, is not now experienced as an eternal presence. It appears unconcealed in its Word-presence in the Scriptures and in the shared word of those who try to follow Christ. In the Word-presence of God's waiting we have a pledge that history is moving towards God's eternal presence in which all things will be subject to him. Now everything is still kept in eschatological suspense. Evil still contradicts God's purpose for man.

Many questions raised by the theology of hope as regards the hermeneutical problem cannot be dealt with in such a brief essay. We must make it clear how we can reinterpret man's Logos in the light of promissory history, that is, how man's reason is related to God's promise. The issues of the historico-critical method are also still with us. With demythologizing it is the same. For example, what do we mean by resurrection? An historical event, a non-historical event, a symbol, or a myth? The linguistic, historical, and ontological status of the affirmations of faith must be clearly articulated, so that men may know what to believe.[27] In

---

27. I wish to stress that the emphasis on theology as eschatology as such does not relieve us from any single historico-critical problem. It offers us a new perspective. But the faithful retelling of the story of faith in strictly historical terms remains a challenge also for this perspective.

the context of what we have said thus far, resurrection appears as hope that God's waiting in Jesus Christ prevails beyond death. But the world as we know it with the inescapable reality of death still contradicts resurrection.

The Politics of the Waiting God

God in his waiting invites us to become his co-workers in transforming the world.

For us, short of the eschaton, there is no other verification of theological language possible than ethical verification. Theology and ethics form a unity: "If any man wills to do [God's] will, he shall know whether the teaching is from God" (Jn. 7, 17). There is no theoretically satisfactory answer to the theodicy question. Why does God let evil and death continue? We do not know. The eschatological emphasis on the "coming God" as the "waiting God" hopes that ultimately God will prevail over evil and death and that the world will reflect his glory. It involves the expectation of the *universal* triumph of God. Ethical verification of God is therefore never found in a merely personal or private good, but in a universal public good that furthers the liberation of mankind from the evils that still haunt it. It is definitely also political. The matrix of the ethical verification is dialectical: no lasting political renewal without personal renewal, and no true personal renewal without political renewal. The theology that seeks to give expression to this dialectic we, together with J. B. Metz and Jürgen Moltmann, can call *political theology*.

In America we owe to Paul Lehmann an ethic of the politics of God. What he meant by that phrase was God's effort of universally making and keeping human life human.[28] It seems an American prefiguration of the theology

---

28. Cf. *Ethics in a Christian Context* (New York, 1963), p. 99.

of hope in the field of ethics. In any case, it involves universally liberating man for being human in the spirit of Jesus Christ. Not as a matter of *imitatio Christi,* of imitation, but of innovation! The newness that broke forth from him can break forth from us in a *new* way. For us today, this primarily means developing the professional skills and the competence for tackling the universal responsibilities of man. The problems of the future are becoming more and more technical problems, to be handled in scientific or scholarly analysis. Here we have our task cut out for us.

A timely way of arguing through the nature of competency in the light of the politics of God is the present theological debate about revolution.[29] Revolution is a slippery word and can be applied to a wide range of changes, from a new line in the ladies' garment trade to a political uprising in Honduras.[30] Its use in theology today points to the conscious attempt of man to break through the straitjacket of convention and to shape his own destiny in reshaping the structures of society. But the breakthrough often comes without a grasp of the dynamics and limits of revolution.

Albert Camus in *The Rebel* has said: "Rebellion cannot exist without a strange form of love."[31] Political theology agrees, but sees this relationship in the light of the dialectic between God's politics and God's waiting. It is occasionally said that today's revolutionaries do not have a blueprint for the society they want to shape, and usually operate with the idea: if we think something is bad, why can't we destroy it, even though we might not know what to put in its place? Revolutionary action occasionally does not have the time to reflect on what lies beyond the liberation from the oppressive conditions of the present. But even in this situation the

29. From the avalanche of recent literature on the subject one example must suffice, Carl Oglesby and Richard Shaull, *Containment and Change* (New York, 1967).

30. Crane Brinton, *The Anatomy of Revolution* (New York, 1965), p. 4.

31. (New York, 1956) p. 304.

revolutionary cannot do without a strange form of love, a grasp of his solidarity with all who are drawn into the effects of revolutionary action, the oppressor as well as the oppressed. Revolutionary action without a strange form of love will be selfish and blind. Political theology, pressed on by God's waiting, perhaps the strangest form of love, will wish, even in the face of the most oppressive circumstances and even while trying to shake them off, to discover the most viable future. The hazardous guess must be eliminated. So we are compelled to plan for the future. Here lies the major task of political theology.

It involves mapping out the difficult road of *non-violent revolution,* a change in society that can leave an opening for a strange form of love. It involves projecting new structures of justice among men who still remain immoral. It involves thinking through the problem of love and justice once more, but now with a new emphasis on the possibilities of newness provided by God, possibilities for social change and renewal.

Planning, however, again creates new laws and conventions, new straitjackets. God's waiting[32] in turn invites us ever anew to break through our best planning and to see the neighbor as the person he is and to find ever new forms of encountering him and urging him on towards God. Beyond all planning lies the unplanned, the unexpected, the new.

I had to be brief in my last point. I did not want to describe a program, but point out a direction. We are living in a time of metanoia, of turning around, of new directions, new leases on life. Memories of darkness still haunt our thoughts: Stalingrad, Auschwitz, the Battle of the Bulge, Hiroshima, Pusan, and now still Khe Sanh. But there is also a new measure of hope. As we arise to new tasks, and also to new tasks in theology, we may begin to see our main direction, so that we, too, can say: "I will arise and go to my father," go towards the waiting God.

32. The recent publication of Karl Barth, *Action in Waiting* (Rifton, 1969), may help to clarify the theological use of "waiting."

THE PROBLEM OF CONTINUITY
Harvey Cox

Once in a while a book drops into our lives that makes a considerable difference in the way we think and the way we act. In 1947, when I was a freshman in college, someone handed me a book entitled *Moral Man and Immoral Society,* and I really have not been the same since. About 1952, I remember sitting up all night spellbound reading *The Courage To Be.* And then rather late in the game, perhaps it was in 1958, I read *Letters and Papers From Prison.* The same kind of thing happened in 1966 with a book entitled *Theologie der Hoffnung:* a basic reorientation in my thinking, a challenge to look at a whole range of problems from an entirely new perspective, a kind of refreshing change in direction. In the two years since the reading of that book and in having gotten to know Professor Moltmann personally. I am not without some questions for him, some doubts which have crept in along the way, and I am now almost ready for another book, although according to my schedule it will at least be 1971 before that happens next.

Perhaps some of the problems of the theology of hope and of Professor Moltmann's thought can best be illuminated by comparing the challenge which he brings to our traditional orientation in theology to the challenge brought by that other most interesting and perhaps notorious movement, the so-called radical movement in American theology, hoping that the contrast might help us to see where the issues lie. Before that, however, a more basic historical, stylistic, and perhaps also methodological question about Moltmann's work should be raised.

It struck me recently that one of the things underlying almost all theological work, including the work that Moltmann does, is an assumption that to demonstrate anything one must demonstrate its *continuity* with some aspect of the Christian theological tradition. That is, the assumption that we must prove our continuity with the tradition is universal in theology, no matter how radical it is, no matter how novel or spectacular. To dispute this assumption that we have to demonstrate in some way that what we say is in some continuity with what has been said before is to leave the dialogue.

Is this assumption of continuity a part of the story of the origin and development of doctrine in Christianity itself? I think it is. In fact, the question of how and why dogma actually began in Christianity is one which used to be asked very frequently in theology, though it is not asked very often nowadays. It was of great interest, as you recall, to Albert Schweitzer, who suggested that the failure of the parousia to occur in early Christianity led to the most profound crisis in the history of the church, in its need to adjust to living somehow in the world that was not in fact replaced by the new age. Then in his *History of Dogma,* Harnack held that the origin of dogma in Christianity is to be attributed to the hellenization of Christianity, a process which Harnack himself lamented. Martin Werner, in his book *The Formation of Christian Dogma,* labels this whole process de-eschatologization. Werner argues that, although the early Christians looked to the future, the imminent kingdom, for a solution to earthly problems, the failure of the parousia to arrive gradually undermined this hope. And this hope was replaced by an attempt to cope with the same problems of living by tracing their origins. Eschatology looked to the future for help in grappling with the present issues of life. Dogma looked to the past for the wisdom and revelation which was mediated through the church in the apostolic succession. Dogma examines the origins of things, Werner claims, and validates its solutions by demonstrating that these answers are in continuity with the answers given by a previous generation of church fathers.

If you take the word hellenization (of Christianity) which Harnack used, or the word de-eschatologization which Werner used, and you think of two figures in contemporary theology, namely, Leslie Dewart and Jürgen Moltmann, Dewart is talking about the dehellenization of theology and Moltmann about its re-eschatologization. So it is very important today, I think, to remember the historical conditions under which our preoccupation with continuity began. If we accept for the moment that it is at least in part the result of the de-eschatologization of Christian theology, that is, if our interest in continuity results from the de-eschatologization of theology, then our present emphasis on the recovery of eschatology, as evidenced in the work of Moltmann, may imply a crisis in modern theology which is much deeper than the one which we had first imagined. That is, can you re-eschatologize and still emphasize continuity, and at the same time give the kinds of arguments for your position that Professor Moltmann does? The reassertion of eschatology raises questions of theological method that even its most articulate spokesman, Professor Moltmann, has not yet dealt with adequately, at least to my knowledge.

The theologians of hope in their various ways are urging what I am calling a re-eschatologization of theology. Each one stresses the need to emphasize the future of the kingdom of God, the eschatological posture. Here we can think of Karl Rahner, Johannes Metz, Wolfhart Pannenberg, and Gerhard Sauter as well as Jürgen Moltmann. They wish to rethink everything in view of the dawn of the new day. Eschatology is not simply one among the doctrines. It is, in terms of a musical figure, the key in which everything else is composed.

The problem with this is a serious one, I think. These theologians pursue the task of re-eschatologization within methodological assumptions which arose as the result of de-eschatologization, the process which they now seek to overthrow. They exhibit, therefore, an unexamined and perhaps an unconscious contradiction at the very basis of their work, a contradiction which will severely limit the extent to which their program can be successfully carried through. One cannot, in my opinion, reëstablish the preëminence of eschatology in Christian thought and still cling to the principle of continuity as the basic rubric in which theological arguments are validated. Let me repeat it, because it is really the thesis of my critique, but now as a question: how can one reëstablish the preëminence of eschatology in Christian thought and still cling to the principle of continuity in one's argument, that is, by demonstrating the validity or by trying to persuade us of the validity of one's arguments by appealing to continuity, if it is true that this whole method of arguing in theology arose as a result of the de-eschatologizing process? Our preoccupation with continuity is a result of or, at least, in part a result of the derogation of eschatology, if Werner and Harnack and Schweitzer can be believed. Thus the methodological approach of the current crop of re-eschatologizers or theologians of hope will inevitably mitigate against the insight they are attempting to reëstablish.

If this is true, we come to an even more difficult question. What if contemporary theologians become aware of this contradiction between what we might call the eschatological and the dogmatic approach to theology, what if they were to become as thoroughly eschatological in their method and style as they insist we should be in our theological content? Then what problem would arise? Obviously, the first question would be: how does one legitimate a theological argument that does not seek to establish its credentials through appeals to one of the forms of continuity, that is, if we cannot claim that a given theological argument is really a demythologized form of Luther or a further development of Thomas, or what Augustine would really have said had he read Freud, or one of the other fictions of continuity which theologians are so good at inventing? If we cannot use any of these devices to demonstrate continuity, then how do we legitimate a theological claim? This is a very knotty problem. Perhaps Professor Moltmann will try to answer it himself.

The problem may not be as difficult if we remember that I am not here suggesting that the entire catalogue of traditional Christian doctrines must now be rethought without any reference whatever to past formulations. That would be a kind of non-historical or a-historical presentism that no one would want to defend. The fact is that the catalogue of traditional theological problems, Christology, ecclesiology, and so on, is itself a product of the dogmatic tradition. The seminary catalogue has a history that exhibits a pattern of development. It cannot be thought of as in any way fixed or eternal. The chapter titles in books on systematic theology are not timeless forms laid up in the mind of God, neither are the divisions into which courses in theology in the seminary curriculum are divided. Now, if the rebirth of the eschatological dimension *is* the great new fact of theology today, and if it helps to deliver us from our constricting obsessions with mere continuity and past orientation, as Professor Moltmann claims it does, then it should deliver us also from the traditional catalogue of theological concerns, and this paradoxically includes a concern for eschatology, a concern for eschatology as one item, among others, in the catalogue of doctrines, however central and however determinative. A rebirth of eschatology which would free us only to become preoccupied with the doctrines of eschatology would not be a liberation at all, but a subtle new form of imprisonment, and indeed an imprisonment in the past.

The eschatological emphasis in theology delivers us hopefully not to an obsessive interest with eschatology, but to a free responsibility for the future as the church moves forth towards that future in authentic hope. Just as the periodic outbursts of interest in eschatology in past history have always threatened the security of the institutional church and have often been dealt with quite severely for just that reason, so the present renewal of interest in eschatology could threaten the whole structure of traditional theology. The re-eschatologizers may have lit a time bomb in the basement of the theological enterprise, a time bomb that is already ticking away. What is more, they may have lit a time bomb unknowingly, a time bomb which will demolish their structure along with everyone else's. They have introduced a dimension which, if it is really pursued in all its ramifications, may not just enrich the theological discourse, but give it a new direction. They are suggesting that the future which God makes possible for man and for his world is the appropriate object of theological inquiry. This will inevitably have revolutionary consequences. It means that the future rather than the past poses the problems we deal with in theology. Imagine what that would do to the theological curriculum!

We occupy ourselves, it suggests, not with the refinement of traditional dogmas, but with the issues posed for man in his political future, in his one political future, and therefore the issues posed to the church, by the need to remain alive, free, human, and loving tomorrow, next month, and next year. This does not mean that we ignore the past, or that the way we have traditionally organized theological concerns, such as Christology, pneumatology, and so on, is altogether outmoded. It does mean, I should think, that we utilize the theological traditions in a different way. We utilize them to think about present and future concerns, whatever they may be—race, war, family, or technology. Just as the concerns of the late twentieth century are forcing a new interdisciplinary organization on the traditional structure of the university, with urban study centers and technology centers and area study centers, maybe the same thing will be required in theology.

If theology is really the theory of historical practice, as Professor Moltmann thinks it is, then all that Professor Moltmann has said so far is prolegomena. Now that he has proven to us that theology can be done in the contemporary world about the future, his next job is to do it, and perhaps our next job too.

Eschatology has to do with the future. Its assertions, therefore, cannot simply be legitimated by appeals to the past, however inventive. Only the future itself will validate or invalidate them. This means that they have a different status from the status which theological assertions or doctrines have had in the past. Formerly, we thought we could decide whether or not they were acceptable on the basis of their continuity with the past. Now this no longer seems possible. It means that the doctrines which the faithful are asked to believe, in the sense of holding them to be true —since as eschatological statements they have to do with the future state of human affairs—are in principle provable or disprovable depending on whether the state of affairs actually comes to pass or not, depending on whether they function as they should to awaken and to stimulate new perception. They must therefore be held with an element of provisionality which is not the case with other kinds of creedal statements.

Two remarks about Professor Moltmann's essay in conclusion. First, no doubt, I would have been even more enthusiastic about his work perhaps five or six years ago, or seven or eight years ago, when, involved in a seminar on Barth's *Church Dogmatics* with Professor Paul Lehmann, I was in my intensely kerygmatic stage. I have been spoiled a little since then by some other things which have come into my horizon of thought. And therefore all of this strikes me as very kerygmatic, that is, as extremely Christological at its base. Would it be possible to work out a theology of hope which is built, for example, on the doctrine of creation, in the sense that God creates in every man the capacity to hope, perhaps even as the *imago dei* in man, or a doctrine of the third person of the Trinity, that is, hope linked to creativity with the universal Spirit of God continuing to operate and to stimulate man to hope, to call him to hope even where the kerygma is not present? I say this because of my increasing sensitivity to the difficulty which a Christological theology of any sort, whether it is a theology of hope or any other, has in a world of so many different religions.

Second, if you look at the theology of hope and radical theology, you find that each of them has two sources. Radical theology has its source not only in the perception of certain theologians of the sense of loss in our contemporary spirituality. It also has its roots in the recent history of Protestant theology, in the movement of Christology towards anthropology and in the immanentist movements. The theology of hope also has at least two sources. One is the development from Schweitzer and the early interest in eschatology in this century up until Professor Moltmann. The other is the fact that theologians find themselves in a world in which everyone is interested in the future. The Marxists are interested in the future. The planners are interested in the future. Herman Kahn is interested in the future. Everyone is interested in the future. And so to some extent theologians also have to get interested in the future, so that they can be on the same wave length.

I would like merely to suggest—and not try to devise any theology about it here—that there is another element in our contemporary cultural and indeed religious sensibility which is extremely important, and which both of these movements have overlooked. That element is the sense of comic hope, the note of celebration, of mirth, of joy, of affirmation of life, even of gaiety, even though there does not seem to be much empirical evidence that would support our gaity or celebration in the world around us.

I had a striking experience of this when I accompanied some divinity students to the induction center in Boston for an induction refusal. In fact, they are now beginning to call it the induction refusal center of Boston. Previous induction refusals had been very grim, serious, and scary affairs. Everyone was scared. The army inductors were just as scared as anyone else. At the last one, however, a young man who was refusing his induction, got some of his friends to bring along a rock and roll band, the girlfriends made some bread and passed out jam, balloons were in evidence, miniskirts, and banners, and the whole affair took on the air of a celebration. Something changed. The induction was again refused, the witness against the war was made, the hope for a better world without war and without killing was stated. But, at the same time, something else was stated which seems to be missing both in the theology of hope and especially in the radical theology: a kind of celebrated affirmation of the flesh, a joy in the here and now which does not preclude hope and criticism, a suggestion to those at the induction center and to those involved in the demonstration that when one is celebrating and kissing and loving the flesh, one does not burn it with napalm. I would like to see a theology which is a rediscovery of the celebrative aspects of life, the goodness of the flesh, the wonderful gift of joy, and which at the same time does not become lost in a wallowing in that discovery, but also affirms our hope for the future. I think this is possible. I think there are traces of it in Moltmann's theology. There are a lot more traces of it in Moltmann himself.

THE UNIVERSAL AND IMMEDIATE PRESENCE OF GOD

Langdon Gilkey

Although there are many interesting topics to discuss with as stimulating and original a theologian as Professor Moltmann, we shall try to restrict the scope of this essay to our speech about God and, within this general area, to our language about the presence and activity of God in the *present*. Specifically, if a text is to be cited, it should be Professor Moltmann's remark[1] that "This universal and immediate presence of God is not the source from which faith comes but the end to which it is on the way." We agree that faith does not stem directly from such universal presence alone, and that our *full* apprehension of that presence is (as the medieval doctrine of beatitude always maintained) a useful definition of the goal of redemption. Nevertheless, we will argue that an affirmation of the universal presence of God in the past and in the present as well as in the future is (a) necessary for the theological position which Moltmann himself proposes, since (b) it is essential if any talk about God at all is to be intelligible and consistent. In the process, we shall try to indicate briefly and all too incompletely how such "presence" might be conceived and how it does in fact relate to faith and to the future.

1. *The Theology of Hope* (New York and Evanston, 1967), p. 282.

One might put our initial point in these terms: Far from disposing of "theism," as he calls a theology inclusive of the immediate and universal presence of God, or from even proposing an alternative, this eschatological theology itself depends upon a theistic view of God, for none of its own basic categories are intelligible without precisely the theistic assumption. The opening part of the essay will be concerned to establish this dependence.

First, however, let us note that a doctrine of God's universal presence is *not* equivalent to a "natural theology"—as the examples of Luther and Calvin surely make clear. Second, if the modern rejection of the supernatural and the modern agony about evil make the theistic God dubious, surely the same modern skepticism makes it perilous, not to say useless, to appeal directly to revelation and so to the authority of the New Testament in theology.[2] It is hardly fair to demolish an opponent with weapons of modern skepticism one refuses to use on oneself, especially if those same weapons have rendered biblical authority as incomprehensible to our age as they have an omnipotent ruler of destiny. And surely the assumption of the appealer to biblical authority that "faith" assures him of the truth of the biblical Word and thus achieves a transcendence of doubt is as weak and "unmodern" an answer as is the same stubborn answer of the theist that, despite the evidence, his "faith" assures him of the reality of universal providence. If *faith* can answer doubts about revelation, it can equally settle the theodicy question! *All* our methodologies in theology are in trouble, and it is as meaningless to appeal to revelation in Scripture as to traditional theistic doctrine *if* we once allow ourselves to invoke the authority of the modern spirit, as Professor Moltmann has done against his theological rivals. Biblicism has "triggered" probably as much atheism as has theism, if such a body-count is at all relevant to theological discourse.

2. Jürgen Moltmann, see above, "Theology as Eschatology."

Finally, does it really help to assuage modern questions about theodicy if we move the whole show into the future (as Kant moved it "inside" to counter Galileo and Isaac Newton)? If, as Professor Moltmann insists, God's future "decides what becomes of the present"[3] and "as the power of the future" God works into the present, for the future is in mastery of the present,[4] and if, as he also holds, this mastery of the present by God's future has been the characteristic of continuing time—and so of the past and present as well[5]—then how is even a "future" God, so conceived, relieved of accountability "for everything that takes place in the world"[6] (and of responsibility "for the experiment man"[7]), the theistic responsibility which, according to Moltmann, triggered atheism and so decapitated the theistic deity? The issue of theodicy is thus not an issue of *tense*. If a future God is *not* responsible for the continuing present at all, then by the same token he is not at all effective either, and is therefore quite as irrelevant to the future "new" as he is to the present. If he is to be relevant for the future and so a ground for hope, ultimately, as time passes, his relevance must be for the present as well. Thus, insofar as he is effective *from* the future on the present, as Moltmann says,[8] he then shares responsibility *for* the present, and the problem of theodicy returns for him as well. The issue is thus not one of tense; rather is it on the one hand the issue of the limits of divine responsibility for historical events, from whatever quarter (present or future) the divine effectiveness operates, and on the other hand the issue of the reality of human autonomy or freedom, and so of the genuine openness of the future. We are prepared to argue that modern forms of theism have offered more likely resolutions

3. *Ibid.*, p. 10.
4. *Ibid.*, p. 11.
5. *Ibid.*, p. 14.
6. *Ibid.*, p. 4.
7. *Ibid.*, p. 6.
8. *Ibid.*, pp. 10, 14 f.

to these issues, if merely because they have discussed them directly, than has an eschatological theology which misconceives the issue as a matter of tense. After all, if the dichotomy "God is" and "God is not" poses for theology a fatal debate,[9] then that fatality is not removed by transposing it into the terms of a God who "will be," and who "is coming." For the future can be seen in as atheistic terms as can the present or the past, as a reading of Marx, Lenin, Orwell, or Herman Kahn reveals—the God who "will be" is *also* balanced by the God who "will not be." And thus is any serious theological debate moved back into the present sphere, where alone it can be conducted, that is to say, where alone anything—God, ourselves, or our world—can be known.

Our argument is that this "eschatological view of God" itself depends upon, requires, or entails a theistic view of God, namely, one in which *whatever* forms of ultimacy, power, purpose, and deity are assigned to God in the future must also be assigned to him in the present and the past—so that all the arguments against theism and for the "deity of the future" are either mere storm and fury or else confused and misdirected. This requirement or entailment can be seen, I believe, if we in turn ask three questions: (1) What does "God" add to future possibility, or what sort of divine transcendence is required here? (2) How is this divine transcendence in and for the future, how is this God, *known* by us? (3) What does the word God here *mean;* how and under what conditions is this eschatological language meaningful at all?

(1) What sort of God is required for the "eschatological new" pictured here? That this is not an atheistic or humanistic vision of the future is quite clear from the following points essential to Moltmann's argument: (a) The new does not here arise out of the development of immanent forces, out of the past in its continuity and unfolding effects

---

9. See *ibid.*, p. 10.

on the present and the future; rather is it a *new* creation, "not a possibility *within* the world and its history, but a new possibility *for* the world, for existence, and for history."[10] Thus this form of possibility, impossible for immanence, must, says Moltmann, arise from transcendence: "Only when the world can be understood as contingent creation out of the freedom of God and *ex nihilo* . . . does the raising of Christ become intelligible as *nova creatio*," and only when viewed as the result or work of such radically transcendent power is the "eschatological process" intelligible.[11] The presupposition for the possibility of this sort of radical newness is that the new comes not *merely* out of future unactual possibility mediated through human intentions and so human autonomy—for then no God at all is implied by newness; rather, like original contingent being, this new arises out of a "more than future" transcendence, out of the actual and so present almightiness and purpose of God.[12] The fact that, as Moltmann continually reiterates, God is known to have been transcendent creator *in* or *through* the eschatological event establishes that God as transcendent creator is one of the *presuppositions* of eschatological events. For something is implied by and so known in something else only if it is not a *consequence* of that something else, but a presupposition or condition of it. Consequently, God's power and deity must be present and actual and cannot be, as is often also said here, one of the future consequences or results of eschatological fulfillment —unless that fulfillment is brought about by some other power than God, which Moltmann denies. (b) Furthermore, as is persuasively argued, our knowledge of God, and so our hope for the future, depends on our confidence that this future is the future of Jesus Christ; and in turn *that* future entails the event of his resurrection, again an event

10. *The Theology of Hope*, p. 179; italics added.
11. *Ibid.*
12. See also *ibid.*, pp. 31, 200, 204.

accomplished not merely by immanent forces or by future possibilities, but solely by the almighty power of *God*.[13] Presumably, in like manner the promised return of Jesus is to be accomplished not through immanence or through the power of future possibility, but through the power and the love of God. (c) Finally, as Moltmann insists, eschatology depends ultimately upon the *faithfulness* of God to his promises implied in the resurrection[14]—and faithfulness, as Luther insisted, entails the continuing power to carry out a consistent intention.

These are not unimportant points. God, Moltmann is here saying, is required in an eschatological theology because the radically new—as in the paradigm case of the resurrection—is a possibility neither for historical immanence nor for human capacities. Consequently, it is evident that neither the raising of the dead nor the radically new can happen merely as future possibilities that are mediated to the present through human autonomy, as is the case in "ordinary" history. Such eschatological events exhibit more *ontologically* than the relation of future possibilities to present human intentions, plans, or dreams. Thus they are *not* to be accounted for "secularly," that is, merely by the power of the future over the present—else God be not at all implied, and so not at all known, through the resurrection event. They exhibit necessarily the present unconditioned power of God, and *thus* is God as creator implied for faith in the apostolic witness to the resurrection. Eschatology as here presented presupposes an actual and so present divine transcendence as source of contingent being and so of resurrection life; it implies a divine stability and so fidelity of intention and purpose; and it implies a divine omnipotence in enacting that purpose—and such is surely the skeletal definition of theism. Not a God who "will be," but a God who very much already is, is required here. Why, in the light of the reiterated interdependence of the eschato-

13. See especially *ibid.*, pp. 165, 187, 203 ff.
14. *Ibid.*, p. 85, 116, 143, 204.

logical new and *creatio ex nihilo,* there is such a continual polemic against God as "ground" or as "source,"[15] is incomprehensible to me.

(2) The necessity for the universal and immediate presence of God is also seen in answer to the question, "How do we *know* of God's part in future hope?" Moltmann makes clear that both a natural theological and what he calls an "epiphany" answer to this question are impossible. We cannot know or derive God from a survey of either nature or history (natural theology), nor do we encounter him through a self-revelation in and through his Word. The Bible is not, therefore, the vehicle of the self-manifestation of God;[16] rather, it is a book filled with prophetic and apostolic statements witnessing to historical events and declaring verbal promises.[17] Thus God's presence in the present is seemingly not necessary here. We know of God's power and intention through the *fact* of the resurrection of Jesus (only *God* could do that, as above), and through the *promises* there and elsewhere that "tell" us of his future. God is present in history only as resurrection-event and as promise, *both* referent not to *themselves* as manifesting God in himself, as vehicles of an encounter with God directly, but both referent only to the future as promise. In turn, the resurrection event, on which the knowledge of eschatology depends, is known through the later "appearances" of Jesus to the disciples—though what historical criticism might do to our "knowing" of this the author does not divulge. The appearances themselves are, of course, mediated to us by apostolic statements in the Scriptures. Thus our *entire* knowing of God—since he cannot be known in the present—begins with these apostolic reports.

One cannot help but ask, "Why should we believe these reports?", since there are so many things in Scripture that we do not, in fact, believe. It may be psychologically, but

15. Moltmann, see above, p. 10.
16. Moltmann, The Theology of Hope, pp. 41–58.
17. *Ibid.*, pp. 103, 117, 118.

surely it is not theologically, sound to reply, "But this is what the faith was founded on, and you have, or pretend to have, 'faith'—for surely those who *had* this faith *believed* these reports, but our question is, 'Why should we believe them?'" Calvin broached this question in Book I of *The Institutes,* and declared that neither the beauty of the apostolic language nor the age of the scriptural books was sufficient ground—nor, as Professor Macquarrie argues, can the fulfillment of eschatological promises yet to be realized help very much. Perhaps the authority of *das Wort* in the German theological tradition is sufficient to explain psychologically the authority, for theologians, of these reports, but, as the authority of the church was not sufficient for Calvin, such traditional authority, even in such an impressive theological tradition, is not sufficient when one is asking *theological* questions. Only the immediate presence of the Holy Spirit, said Calvin, can be a basis for faith in these words—and that is an immediacy of the divine which witnesses in our hearts to the truth of this apostolic witness. Otherwise, one might remark, we should in conscience treat these first-century reports of "appearances" as we do the early Buddhist disciples' accounts of Gautama's many miracles.

But even more, Moltmann himself argues our case persuasively when he says that in order for us to regard the resurrection as an intelligible and so possible "historical reality," we must not regard history "as man's history." For on that anthropological presupposition these reports will be to us merely credulous recitations of impossible events and therefore historically meaningless.[18] Thus the *presupposition* for our acceptance of the apostolic witness as credible, and so for our even looking at the resurrection as a possibility, is that we have already in some way transcended the anthropological understanding of history, i.e., that we are aware at least of the possibility of the presence and activity of God in and through that history. Without such a

18. *Ibid.*, p. 134.

prior sense of the divine, of the dimension of ultimacy both in nature and in history, and, I am sure also, without the presence of the Holy Spirit in and through these scriptural words, these reports of post-resurrection appearances will seem to us merely harbingers of an outlandish and primitive world view and hardly heralds of the new age to come! The biblical appearances and the biblical promises are not *available* to us in the twentieth century as bases for our knowledge of God unless the immediate presence of God is in some sense presupposed, establishing their credence.

(3) Finally, we must broach, though we cannot exhaust, the crucial problem of the *meaning* of this eschatological language in theology. It is important to recognize that the question of the meaning of an assertion is a different question from that of its validity. Faith (which as we have just noted *also* requires the presence of God) can presumably certify to the believer the truth of what is believed, that Christ rose, that God will continue to bring in the new, that ultimately the divine promise will be fulfilled. It is impossible, however, for faith alone to certify or provide the meaning of what is thus believed, since that meaning is presupposed as that which faith affirms. And the modern secular accusation is not so much that statements such as these, or that "God's being is future," "God's being is coming," are not *true*, as that they are *meaningless*, that we do not know, and have no way of knowing what is here being said or claimed by them. This issue of meaning, as opposed to validity, is the crux of the contemporary theological problem: it requires that if we are to use unusual noun symbols, such as "God," and ordinary predicate words in unusual ways, such as "God *brings* in the new from the future," "He is the God who *will be*," etc., we give an account of the new usage we are making of these words and so of the meanings we are endeavoring here to express.

Certainly part of the problem in this theology is that a new philosophical interpretation of time, unfamiliar to many of us, is being here presented; I suspect many of the difficulties we have with the notion of the "future determining the present," etc., stem from this as yet unplumbed philosophical viewpoint. But the *theological* problem of meaning does not reside in the mysteries of Ernst Bloch. It centers, rather, around the question what the symbol "God" means or intends within this general point of view about the future and so what these predicate words mean when they appear in "God-sentences," when, for example, we use this word—either in old theistic or in new Blochian sentences—in saying "*God* raised Jesus," "*God's* being is future," and so on.

Now our point is that when we insist—as any theology, eschatological or theistic, must do—that this symbol and so these sentences are meaningful as opposed to meaningless, we are saying that this symbol *means* because it thematizes or brings to clarity some definite aspect of ordinary, present, secular experience. The meaning of a symbol consists in its relation to some region or area of shared experience—else it does not "fit" anywhere in experience at all, and, like a Kantian category without empirical content, is empty and bodiless. The Christian symbol "God" derives, to be sure, from such unique experiences as are referred to in the current phrase, "Word-events" —and thus we agree that faith is not born out of universal experience. But what that symbol *names,* and so what it *means,* is an aspect of general experience, else the symbol itself has no sharable meaning for any of us. The possibility of "Word-events" as meaningful, and especially of the language in which they are communicated, lies in the fact that religious language as a whole has reference to certain definite, universally present ranges of experience which this language *means,* and about which it can communicate. Meaning is the interaction of symbol and shared experience —and even eschatological symbols, symbols referent to the transcendent in the future—are dependent for the meaning of their transcendent symbolic elements on the present presence in general and shared experience of a dimension of ultimacy to which these symbols refer and which they each, in their own unique way, name.

Without this ground for theological meaning, theological words are empty of content. They carry at best only traditional meanings, and thus new definitions, as in this case, will only compound the problem: Who or what is the *God* whose being is only future, and how might we know? Where is the situation in experience where this word is appropriately used, so that we can begin to feel what it might mean? And unless one assumes that this possibility is given *in toto* with the Word in an epiphany revelation of both its meaning and its validity, as Barth did, we must locate this "ground" for the meanings of theological symbols in some aspect of general experience. To deny at one fell swoop *both* the revelationist *and* the anthropological bases for the meaning in experience of theological symbols is to leave them with at best only emotive, nostalgic content—which is just what much of our present traditional biblical and doctrinal theological language does. The presence of God, apprehended as a dimension of ultimacy, qualifying all that we are and do, is required—so I believe—if religious language and so our Christian theological symbols (theistic or eschatological) are to have meaning to us, just as a vivid *experience* of that presence (what we call "faith") is required if what we say with this language is to claim validity. We argued above that the special presence of God in revelation is necessary for the sense of the *validity* of theological affirmations; now we are arguing that the *universal* presence of God in experience generally is necessary if theological assertions are to have *meaning*. Theism in some form is a requisite presupposition of any intelligible Christian theology. This is especially true in an eschatological theology where our only relation to God is through verbal theological symbols. That is to say, since, as Moltmann argues, God here contradicts most of present experience,[19] and does not manifest *himself* in any present epiph-

19. *Ibid.*, pp. 18, 35, 86.

any, and as a consequence can be related to only through his "verbal promises," that is, through some sort of meaningful theological symbolization, only in the future will God be immediately there for us. Now we can know him only *symbolically,* through verbal promises, and thus the question of meaning and of the relations of verbal symbols to experience has a decisive importance in this theology.

Another aspect of the problem of meaning centers, as we noted, around the new philosophical vision incorporated into this theology. I have only the most skimpy knowledge of Ernst Bloch, but I gather that some of the most important ontological characteristics of the eschatological God Moltmann recommends have their source in Bloch's philosophy. For unless we understand the unique and original way Bloch comprehends the relation of the future to the present, we cannot understand Moltmann's theological assertions. Apparently for Bloch the future moves into, impinges upon, "masters," and even "decides about" the present.[20] The future affects the present in terms of possibility, dreams, visions, promises—all of them, let us note, mediated through the actualized by *human* autonomy. In any case, the continuity of moments is thus determined more by the future's effect on the present than through the past's effect on the present—though there are what are called "tendencies" which mediate the past to the present and into the future. Thus our usual understanding of "historical causality" or effectiveness is here precisely reversed; historical efficacy is not a continuity out of the past, a development of what is already given, a "push" from the given past on the present and so the future. Rather, historical effectiveness moves from future possibility into present human actuality, not from past actuality into future potentiality. This view of the relation of future to the historical present is surely a fascinating expression of many important aspects of the modern spirit: the sense of freedom from the past and of openness to the future with its promises of the new;

20. Moltmann, see above, pp. 10, 13; *The Theology of Hope,* p. 243.

of almost unlimited creaturely autonomy over against the determining structures of fate or destiny (a strange view for a Marxist!); of the loss of given and eternal "essence" as definitive of man and its replacement by "existence" or the power to decide new possibilities.

This analysis of time and its structure, which one must call a "secular" one, since it is not exegetically derived, helps explain crucial segments of Moltmann's theology: how a God whose being is said to be only "future" is thereby not rendered totally irrelevant and ineffective. According to this view of time, God, though only future, does master the present, as does all futurity, and is therefore immensely effective and so significant in that he is the Lord of the future which in turn is lord of the present. What *God* adds to this general, or so to speak "secular," power of the future over the present we have already tried to explain. His radical transcendence and power are necessary that the new be really new, that life arise from death, that hope arise from the nothingness of the present, and so on; and we are, secondly, able to have *hope* only because the future that God has promised is the future of Jesus Christ, dominated by the divine intentionality characterized by the righteousness which wills the redemption of man.

The Christian symbol "God," connoting transcendent power and universal love, adds the possibility of the radically *new* and of the new that is *good* to this Blochian view of the future. It should be noted that an apparent contradiction—or at least two different models—is present here. One model is the effect of future possibility in and through human freedom, in plans and projects; the other is the personal *power* of God who *acts* as creator, not man's possibility of free action, but quite beyond all creaturely capacities, as in the *event* of resurrection. Jesus is raised by *God,* says Moltmann. Nevertheless, it is the purely temporalistic ontology of the latter, and not the first model, that is determinative for the particular futurist form that this eschatological theology proposes in its view of God—and, we shall argue, it is this ontology that causes it to repudiate the very theism it itself requires.

Two points here are relevant to the course of this argument. In the light of this important dependence of this theology on Bloch—in its doctrines of time, of historical continuity, of the relation of present and future, and so of God—I do not know what is meant when it is categorically stated that in theology "We cannot apply to Jesus Christ a concept of history that has been arrived at in terms of other experiences,"[21] or when it is claimed that the development of this theological viewpoint through a study of the Bible does not "imply any general religious-historical perspective."[22] Does this theology *really* think that this view of time, of historical continuity and of the future, is simply "there" in the Bible, and that by good luck (or providence!) Bloch hit on it secularly? How are we to understand or to justify this congruence between secular philosophy and biblical wisdom except in terms of providence, or of the universal and immediate presence of the divine to secular thinkers, as the early and medieval churches justified *their* use of secular philosophy by the heavily-maligned Logos theory?

But more importantly, the history of theology implies that it is always risky to take over a secular philosophy— especially if one is unaware of its influence, and no one is more unaware of such influences than those who feel that their theology is merely biblical. It is risky because it may distort the Christian message by setting too restrictive limits for the resultant theology, limits defined by its own secular viewpoint and so destructive of elements peculiar to the Christian tradition. Most secular philosophies of our time are radically temporalist and futurist; with some qualifications it can be said that, from Bergson and Alexander through Dewey and Whitehead to the early Heidegger at least, reality lies only in change, in the stream of time, in

21. Moltmann, see above, p. 24.
22. Moltmann, *The Theology of Hope*, p. 95.

the movement of passage from past to future. In such a temporalist framework, that which transcends change and temporality seems meaningless, for all there is is the stream of passage. Consequently, if it is agreed, as a revolutionary viewpoint *would* agree, that God is not past as the all-determining genetic power, or present as the universal cause of the ambiguous status quo, then he must be only future as the possibility towards which process is moving. Secularity knows only immediacy, flux, and passage; a *revolutionary* secularity will concentrate its "religious concern" and its commitments only on future possibility—though Marx certainly realized how firmly the future is rooted in the dialectical forces of the past and the present. Secular revolutionary mythology, in other words, will find its deity in the future alone; though the evil past and the godless present belong to the enemy, the future is ours alone!

Whether such a view of an evil past, a God-forsaken present, and a shining future is, or can be, Christian, is a long debate; I doubt it. But that it is secular I have little question. I submit, therefore, that this philosophy provides the real basis for the case Moltmann makes against theism. A view of God who transcends historical passage and so the difference of past and future, while at the same time being involved and active deeply in that passage (in the past, the present, and the future) and who precisely because he is not himself new can bring in the new, is surely not opposed by the biblical view in itself, but only as that view is seen from the perspective of this secular and so purely temporalist philosophy. For the eschatology proclaimed in this theology reflects, as we have shown, not merely the power of future possibility over the present, a power that can be mediated only through the autonomy of man. Rather, that eschatology is grounded in the past act of God in raising Jesus from the dead—something which possibility, mediated through human autonomy, could never do—and so, as Moltmann argues, presupposes the transcendent divine power of the creator of being and the preserver of life. Its hope, correspondingly, is dependent on the faithfulness of God now and forever. Even this biblical eschatology presupposes a God who transcends passage as well as works within it, a God who is, who was, and who is to come. Again, and now on the deepest ontological level, a consistent eschatology calls for a theistic deity.

* * *

Much more difficult and vulnerable than the easy and safe work of criticism is the work of construction. In making intelligible the viewpoint from which the criticism proceeds, one exposes oneself in turn to criticism. Then the imposing critic, who formerly loomed so large, now shrinks in size and, joining his erstwhile victim at the pharmacist's, finds himself purchasing balm for his *own* wounds.

Our critique was based on the assertion that Moltmann's view was too secular, too time-bound, if you will, and therefore not dialectical enough to encompass the dimensions of the biblical eschatology it sought to express. That is, his explicit language about God as the God whose being and deity are future does not provide bases for: (1) the power of God as creator requisite for the act of resurrection and the bringing-in of the radically new in time; (2) for the presence of God in and through his Word and Spirit, that we may now know of this power and intentionality and so be able to hope for the future; and (3) for the *sensus divinum,* as Calvin put it, so that both our questions about destiny and the future, and the divine answers to them, are meaningful to us. A view of deity able to meet these conditions cannot locate God *merely* in the future—the God, not who was and is, but who will be—or see his effectiveness as only the movement of possibility into actuality. Rather, for this conception itself to function, God who thus decides (in part) the future, must also be the ground of past and present *being;* the actual ground of future possibility; thus the ruler (in part) of past and present destiny; and, finally, in some mode or other, a universal and immediate *presence* both in nature and in grace, both generally in human life and history, and specially in particular events, and so in faith through the Word. On the other hand, Moltmann is right to emphasize in his view of deity: (a) the essential relation of God to an open future and so to possibility; (b) the limitation (he makes it a total abdication) of God from the role of an all-determining power of past and present; and thus (c) the role of God in the creation of a new that is really new and as the ground of a genuine transformation of historical reality. As we suggested, the real issue here is not the issue of *tense*. Rather, it is the issue of the dialectical relation of God's universal presence and immediacy as the foundation of all, and as the final determinant of the horizon of our historical being on the one hand, with the radical reality of genuine autonomy, of open possibility for the future, and of a plausible ground for hope in a genuinely unactualized future on the other. Is this dialectic possible or conceivable; or must we settle *either* for an all-determining Absolute of past and present—and so for no new in the future—*or* for a God pushed out—like the Deist God but in the opposite direction—into the relative chill of abstract, because future, possibility? It might be noted that the two current significant forms of theology which are challenging traditional theism are concerned with this same issue, except that they resolve it in different ways. Process theology seeks to open the way to freedom, to possibility, and to the new by setting an *ontological* limit to God, i.e., by conceiving God as a finite factor in the creation of the present; and this eschatological theology in turn sets a *temporal* limit to God, i.e., by conceiving him as infinite and omnipotent, but only in the time that is to come. Is an alternative to these views, which are right in that to which they object but incomplete in what they assert, possible? Is a dialectic of divine presence and yet of absence, of divine presence and yet of human autonomy, of the sacral creativity of the given and yet of the possibility of the radical new, conceivable?

Let us begin with a slight modification of our text: "The universal and immediate presence of God is not the source from which faith comes; but it is something of which we are continuously but dimly aware, it is the basis of the peculiar characteristics of our humanity, and it is the ground in general experience for the meanings of the special language of faith; and its full realization in consciousness and in commitment is assuredly the end to which faith is on the way."[23] The concluding part of this essay will be an exegesis of this amended text, an exegesis which, in relation to the problem with which this essay is concerned, contains three major principles or assertions.

(1) The humanity of man—both his creative powers and his demonic capacities, his joys and his anxieties—stems from the dimension or horizon of ultimacy and sacrality in which he exists, a dimension or horizon which can be and is experienced in a multitude of ways and thematized through a wide variety of "religious" symbols, both negative and positive. The presence of this dimension of ultimacy and sacrality is the ground for the meaningfulness of religious discourse, for it provides that region of ordinary experience, that "situation" in ordinary life in which these symbols are appropriately used, which they thematize and bring to clarity, and which they can be said, in part at least, to "mean." Only if theological symbols, including eschatological ones, are expressive (in their own way) of these ranges of experience in ordinary life, do they mean anything; for meaning, even for the future, arises from the interaction of symbol and present experience.

(2) Faith, and thus a *Christian* meaning of the sacred and ultimate as "God," arises out of definite, particular manifestations and so experiences of the sacred *in* a particular historical community, and so *through* a particular set of symbols, both existent or "real" symbols and verbal ones. Christian faith and language represent *one* of the many perspectives through which the ultimate and sacral

23. *Ibid.*, p. 282.

ground and structure of things is viewed; they are *unique* in the way in which the mystery of the sacred is interpreted, named, and related to. Christian faith thus has its origin in what it calls the Word, and it issues in its own unique orientation to past, present, and future and its own unique forms of hope. But the meaning and the relevance of what it believes and that for which it hopes have their foundation in the universal human awareness of ultimacy, in the human apprehension of the sacred and the holy. The problem of ultimate meanings in life and in history and the universal anxiety concerning the possibility of ultimate meaninglessness provide the *meaning* for eschatological symbols. Such problems and anxieties arise out of our situation within a context of ultimacy of which we are dimly aware, i.e., in the secular questions of significance amidst relativity and insignificance, of hope amid the possibility of despair, of justice amid rampant injustice; and these questions, characteristic of human existence per se, arise out of man's intrinsic relatedness to his context of ultimacy. *Because* he is already and continuously in relation to "God"—else this dimension not be there at all—*therefore* is man a creature of meaning and of freedom, and so is his freedom in time both blessed and plagued by the questions of justice, of the future, and of hope. Without this base, the promises of the Word and man's responding hopes for the parousia would not "fit" anywhere in his experienced world, and so would have no meaning and thus no importance to him. This correlation of anthropology (and so of the continual presence of God to man) with the eschatological Word is tacitly assumed by Professor Moltmann when he appeals, as the ultimate grounds of his argument,[24] both (a) to the sense for the new and the future and to the importance of the category of hope in modern *secular* man's feeling for life, and (b) to the presence of eschatological hope as the

24. Cf. *ibid.*, and Jürgen Moltmann, "The Category of the New in Christian Theology," in Maryellen Muckenhirn (ed.), *The Future as the Presence of Shared Hope* (New York, 1968), pp. 10, 23 ff.

unique *biblical* theme. This tacit correlation between secular experience and biblical witness in his argument points to an *ontological* correlation between (a) the hidden presence of God to man generating religious questions of meaning, justice, and hope in time and a multitude of religious answers, and (b) the symbolic perspectives on that presence and that future expressive of the biblical tradition.

(3) A Christian doctrine of God, therefore, is a "naming" of this hidden and yet manifest presence of ultimacy and sacrality by means of the symbols of this community, the community in which these pressing questions of our being in contingency and in time have been clarified and resolved. The experiences within the range of ultimacy—experiences of our contingency, of our searching for meaning now and in the future, of valuing and decision-making, of alienation and guilt, of the hope for forgiveness and a new being, for renewal and for a new world—these experiences, characteristic of all secular life and yet generated by our continual relation to ultimacy, form the "stuff" with which the Christian symbols have to do. The symbols of creation, of providence, of the Logos, of the divine law, of judgment, of mercy, forgiveness, grace, and the eschatological promises of fulfillment have *religious* meaning insofar as they thematize, clarify, and so are understood in terms of these ordinary but crucially significant experiences. Without the particular symbolic forms, the secular experience of sacrality is unarticulated because unthematized, and the secular anxieties about the Void and the demonic are unconquered because unclarified and unresolved. On the other hand, without the "matter" of some aspect or range of ordinary experience, symbolic statements about God—especially eschatological ones pertaining only to the future—remain only abstract and empty because unrelated to experience. The presupposition of any meaningful language about God is thus the continual and immediate presence of the divine in present experience. The presupposition of valid language about God is that the vagueness (and am-

biguity) of the sacred as apprehended in ordinary experience is clarified by "true" symbols, i.e., for Christians by symbols expressive of this community's experience of and reflection on the activity of God as mediated to it in its past and present and hoped-for in its future. Needless to say, the thorny issues, quite unexplored in the above, concerning what validity means and how it is established in relation to religious symbols, are quite beyond the reach of this essay. In any case, Christian words about God, Christian "meanings," combine the generality and universality of ordinary, secular experience and the particularity of Christian symbolism—and correspondingly a Christian doctrine of God will include, along with that which is hoped-for on the basis of the divine promises, also words about that real and yet hidden presence of the divine which qualifies all our existence as human and makes religious language meaningful to us.

If all this is so, then a statement about *how* God is present in the present—which is what we are required to try to make if we would adequately challenge Moltmann's denial of God's presence—would combine two elements: (1) a description of how that presence is dimly, vaguely, and with utter ambiguity apprehended in secular experience as the basic qualification of our humanity and as the fundamental ground for the meaningfulness of all religious language; and (2) in a very preliminary fashion, a description of how that hidden and yet manifest presence is to be named, understood, and talked about from the point of view of Christian faith, that is, in positive, theological discourse structured in terms of Christian (biblical and traditional) symbols. That this latter theological amplification is also complicated by the inevitable use of ontological and so philosophical categories—as Moltmann used the categories of Bloch—there can be no question.

How is the divine apprehended in the present, not from the point of view of faith, but as the qualification of ordinary human existence? In order to answer this question, a phenomenological hermeneutic of secular experience (*not* of "Word-events," let us note) is required as a kind of prolegomenon to Christian theological language about God. Such a hermeneutic will, we believe, bring to light that each level or aspect of man's being in the world receives its human character by a dimension or horizon of ultimacy within which that aspect functions and is experienced. Man is *man* because both his world and his own autonomous powers, that which is "given" to him, and the intelligence and freedom with which he deals with that given, are set within a context of ultimacy. Let us note that in each case ultimacy appears in secular existence as much negatively as positively, as the hiddenness of the sacred and so as the Void, as well as the creative presence of the sacred. This is the ambiguity that renders impossible a natural theology based on general experience, that accounts for the valid emphasis on the "hiddenness" of God in the Christian tradition, and that drives all Christian theology towards an eschatological fulfillment.

(1) Man experiences his *contingency* and fragmentariness, his own being, in relation to a context of ultimacy; and both his love and celebration of his life—and his flesh—and his anxiety about its loss—and consequently his secular behavior as a contingent being—cannot be understood without an appreciation of his awareness through his experience of his own contingency of this dimension of ultimacy, be it experienced as the Void of fate or as the wonder of sacred being.

(2) Man searches for *meaning,* both in the present and in the future also in such a context of ultimate meaning; that is, he experiences his own *relativity* or insignificance in space and time against a horizon that is not relative. Both the ultimate Void of meaninglessness and the buoyancy of Eros and of hope are alike misunderstood unless this dimension within which his own relativity is apprehended is seen. The biblical eschatological language, which speaks about the hopefulness or hopelessness of history, about the

dread of meaninglessness or a confidence in promises of the new, has no meaningful lodgement in experience and so in discourse unless this ordinary consciousness of history, and so of our immersion in it, is experienced *religiously,* i.e., as related to a dimension of ultimacy and sacrality which *we* name as God.

(3) Man seeks to *know* his world and himself, and in that inquiry he searches for what is valid, for a knowledge that is not merely relative and so subject to ultimate doubt. And this enterprise of knowing is also exercised and apprehended in a context of ultimacy, where both doubt and a false absoluteness are equally real threats, and where creativity is only possible when our relative powers of knowing are related to an ultimate commitment to truth, an ultimate and controlling affirmation of norms, and an apprehension of a virtually unconditioned certainty which makes relative judgments possible.[25]

(4) Man makes *decisions* about his life and so inescapable judgments of value. However relative these decisions and even these norms may be, they function as absolute in the existence of each man who affirms them in decision, and thus themselves presuppose a context or dimension of ultimacy. Like his intelligence, man's very freedom relates him to a moral ultimacy and sacrality, experienced as the "ideal" or the "ought," by which his freedom guides and directs itself.

(5) Universally, man's freedom fails to enact the values it chooses. Here again, universally, ultimacy is experienced, but now not as moral lure or as ideal, but as an ultimate condemnation. As a result, alienation, from self and others, and guilt are known in all personal experience in both religious and secular life; and, correspondingly, external or historical community is universally experienced as broken and diseased, and objective history as unjust, depraved, dead, and God-forsaken. The penitent for sin and the

---

25. Cf. the writings on this issue of Thomas Kuhn, Stephen Toulmin, Michael Polanyi, and B. J. F. Lonergan.

prophet against social wrong, the healer of the person and the reforming revolutionary of social history, all presuppose this apprehension of ultimate condemnation, experienced through the subjective and the objective distortion of our moral freedom and its values. Neither the language of social revolution vis-à-vis justice and righteousness nor the eschatological language of confident hope in and through the condemnation of the moral law and related to the ultimate context of historical possibility is presupposed.

(6) Finally, man, having experienced ultimacy through his own sin and his own temporality, seeks (a) an ultimate reconciliation and justification, both within himself and with his neighbor, and so for a new being and a new world; and (b) that which can overcome the final threat of death. These are not so much based on "religious" experiences, as if man knew them only in church or when hearing proclamation—one does not have to be religious to experience the Void of guilt or of death. They are rather universal and secular, and they provide the themes of most secular drama and give rise to the problems with which most secular mythology deals.

At each level of our human existence a Void is experienced which has the character of ultimacy because in it our powers are engulfed; there is nowhere to stand, no basis for creative reaction, and so no hope of self-renewal. Correspondingly, on the positive side an experience of ultimacy as positive is an apprehension of that which grounds and so establishes our powers, and therefore that which we neither have created nor can control. Again such apprehensions, in serenity, creativity, and hope, or in anxiety, self-hatred, and despair, are the premises in experience for the meaningfulness of the classic Christian symbols of the divine law and judgment, and of God's love and forgiveness, of grace and renewal, of resurrection and of eternal life, and of the final eschatological fulfillment. None of this language would have meaning, because man would not be man, without the universal and immediate presence of God apprehended by our freedom in terms of the dimension of ultimacy and sacrality, a dimension whose true character is often obscured and so which is experienced as much negatively as Void, condemnation, and death as it is positively in joy, serenity, meaning, and courage. To bring the divine in at the last eschatological minute as a total stranger to a world formerly devoid of his presence is (a) to mistake God's presence for our full *knowledge* of his presence, (b) to misread the human situation as *secular* and not as *religious* in its fundamental present character, (c) to overlook the structure of ultimacy that characterizes our apprehension of ourselves and of history and so our present experience both of despair and of hope, and (d) to make the divine promises centered about the Word unrelated to our experience and so to our meaningful use of linguistic symbols.

An ambiguous but very significant dimension of ultimacy and sacrality is, therefore, experienced as the basis for our being in the world, and so for all our passive and our active dealings with it; and, correspondingly, it is the basis for the way in which we apprehend our being in time, our search for meaning and justice, and so the whole question of our hopes for the future. This general presence of the divine provides the occasion in ordinary experience, if not the appropriate Christian forms, for their explication, for eschatological symbolization. To explicate this dimension as secularly apprehended is the task of a *prolegomenon* to theology, but not a part of theology itself.

Now to move on to positive theology. If we are to talk of this universal presence in its relation to eschatology, not from the perspective of our secular apprehension of it—which is ambiguous, negative as well as positive, and therefore hopelessly undetermined—but from the perspective of Christian faith and so theologically in terms of Christian symbols, how *then* do we describe it—when, to recall Calvin's symbolism, we have put on the spectacles of the Word and now see more clearly what before was hidden and confused? How does the universal and immediate presence of God appear, not in a prolegomenon to theology, but in systematic theology itself?

Almost every fundamental aspect of man's being and correspondingly, every major Christian symbol, is relevant to the relation of the universal presence of God to eschatology; this was the crux of our critique in the first part that Moltmann's eschatology itself implied the symbols of creation, of preservation and providence, and of general as well as special revelation. For man experiences the passage of time into the future, the impingement of possibility upon the present, and the call to refashion the world according to justice and love—the main categories of eschatology in Moltmann's view—as *already* a religious being; that is, as a contingent being menaced by fate (and so in relation to the symbol of creation) as in search of meaning (and so in relation to providence), as under ethical norms (and so in relation to the divine will), as guilty and alienated (and so in relation to the divine judgment), and finally in search of forgiveness and reconciliation, and of a new world and a new age (and so in relation to the divine love and the divine promises of fulfillment). To specify in Christian terms, therefore, how God acts in the present in preparation for his "coming"—for the deity that "will be" —would be a rehearsal of the doctrinal meanings inherent in the symbols of creation, providence, judgment, grace, and promise—not to mention that of the divine Logos, through which all that is known by man is known. All we can do at the conclusion of this essay is to attempt to illumine two points in this wide expanse: the dialectic of divine ultimacy and human autonomy, and the dialectic of present providential actuality and future possibility. For the dilemma of Moltmann's theology, it seems to me, lies centrally in that he feels that in order to safeguard the second term of each pair, he must deny the first—or at best move it out of the present and into the future.

Our point, on the other hand, is that there is no human

autonomy—either in cognitive inquiry or in moral decision—without a context or dimension of ultimacy. Thus the divine ultimacy—which founds, limits, and rescues the present—is not "unconditioned" or absolute in the sense that it determines human autonomy, and thus every last character of what is in time. Rather, it is that on which our *real* contingency, our *real* relativity, our *real* freedom, and the *real* openness of life and of history depend; it is the context within which they function, found because *they* are there and thus not capable of dissolving them and remaining intelligible. For ultimacy appears precisely within the exercise of our contingent being, the discovery of our relative meanings, the achievement of our relative truths, the enacting of our relative and free decisions, and so on, as their possibility, as the dimension or context that makes them possible. The presence of God as the dimly apprehended source of our being, the context of our meanings, the inspirer of our values, and the standard by which we experience judgment, does not mean at all that all that we will, he also wills. Nor does it mean that all that is reflects his unalterable intentionality, so that God is responsible for all that is, and that we or history are incapable of producing anything genuinely new. The absoluteness of God as we seek to comprehend it is precisely *not* a necessity that smothers our contingency, nor is it an absoluteness over against our autonomy; rather is it their ground and limit, their context, that which is implied or presupposed in their apprehension and exercise. In this ultimacy, therefore, there is both dynamic and reciprocity; all that is required is that it be so symbolized that it is (a) creative of our being and our freedom; (b) beyond our creation, our control, and our determination; and so (c) able in its negative forms to threaten and as positive to rescue our capacities when they founder. In this sense of ground, limit, and resource—and in that sense alone—God is ultimate. God as creator and as providential ruler is thus not only essentially active, present, and creative of the new, but also essentially self-limiting, producing a free, contingent being that is not himself and whose actions are not his actions—but a creature which can neither be, be in time, value, know, judge, nor have meaning and hope without its relation to God's being, his intentions, his meanings, and his love.

The same sort of claim must be made about the relation of actuality to possibility, namely, that as autonomy depends on ultimacy, so historical possibility is dependent finally on divine actuality in some form. As Whitehead has rightly said, possibility must be somewhere, and the "somewhere" must be present else it be not at all. Thus the very possibility of openness, of the new, of the radically better, does not deny the presence of God in and to the present; it requires it. The providence of God, we may say, is the prerequisite, not the antithesis, for eschatology, for both the divine promise and the parousia of God. God's actuality must span present and future, knowing what has already been actualized by freedom and envisioning what may be actualized by freedom in the moments to come. The reasons for this requirement of a *present* providential envisioning of future possibility may be briefly stated: For there to be present creaturely freedom, there must be a new that is genuinely possible, i.e., that is both *unactual* in the present and yet in some *relation* to what now is. Consequently, there must also be a lodgement of that possibility, *as possible,* in present actuality; that possibility must now *be* somewhere, and it must also be in some mode of *continuity* as well as in discontinuity with the present. In Christian symbolism that "where," where possibility now is, and is in some structural or intentional relation to actuality, is in the envisioning power of the divine providence, which directs and limits the relation of possibility to the actual present as actuality moves into the future. This relation of the new in the future to the actuality of the present in terms of an ultimate context of possibility presently rooted in God's universal vision and his intentions is *one* way of conceiving of present providence which both grounds ultimacy and maintains openness. For in such a concept the context of ultimacy within which we experience personal, social, and historical meanings, the relation of present to future hopes, the relation of present actuality to future possibility, and yet the freedom of the future from the absolute determination by the past and the present, are all explicated. A concept of providence as the divinely envisioned ultimate context of possibility precludes neither the appearance of the radically new nor the autonomous freedom of creatures. For God's possibilities know only the bounds of his good purposes and the limits of relevance. Even the radically new of the resurrection, which brought life out of death, was *relevant* to the perennial problem of transience; it reëstablished an everlasting life *analogous* to life at present, and it promised a future *similar* in quality to the love and righteousness of the *historical* Jesus of the Gospels. A *totally* new future of the resurrection would never have appeared as in continuity with Jesus or have held any promise for the sufferings and trials of life as we know it. The newest of redemptive possibilities, if it holds promise for the fulfillment of what we now are, must have continuity as well as discontinuity with our present fragmentary, guilty, but hopeful selves. And the promised "new" in social history, if it is to be *historical* and if it is to have *promise* for our situation, must be prepared within, relevant to, and fulfilling of what is now the actual in the world around us. We can only hope for that which is different from but also relevant, both negatively and positively, to what now is—else all divine judgments and all divine promises be meaningless to us and ineffective around us. The future which God brings presupposes the present which he also providentially founds—and both require for their actualization our human creaturely and often wayward autonomy, energy, commitment, faith, *and* activity.

ESCHATOLOGY AND TIME
John Macquarrie

In spite of all the multiplicity and diversity of contemporary thought, one constant factor that seems to run through most of it is a preoccupation with the notion of time. This would be true of the natural sciences. Nineteenth-century physics envisaged the atom as a solid particle occupying a minimal space, but as soon as it was recognized that the atom is a dynamic energy system rather than a solid particle, it became clear that it needs a minimum amount of time as well as of space in which to exist. Biology always did have a more intimate relation to time because life itself takes place in time, but with the theory of evolution time took on a larger role and it became possible to understand nature not as a static order but as a vast movement in which everything is affected by change and development, or, in some cases, decay. One could make similar points about other sciences, and what is true of the sciences is also true of the major types of philosophy in the twentieth century. Those philosophies which begin from nature as it is disclosed in modern science make much of the categories of evolution and process, as in writers like Bergson, Alexander, and Whitehead. Philosophies like existentialism which begin from man speak of the temporality of human existence and of the historical nature of thought itself. Even the concept of being, traditionally opposed to the concept of becoming, has itself in contemporary ontologies been set in motion and related to the horizons of time and history.

The new emphasis on time really amounts to something like a revolution in Western thinking because, from the period of Plato or even earlier, priority has been given to that which is timeless and eternal and there has even been a suspicion, made explicit in some philosophers right down until recent years, that time is an illusion. On this view, we see things truly only if we see them *sub specie aeternitatis*. Even when an idealistic type of philosophy had declined, the old suspicion of time lingered on. Western thinking continued to be dominated by the category of substance, understood usually as inert thinghood; and mathematics, which deals in eternal unchanging truths, was taken to be the paradigm of the sciences.

The revolution in thinking as time asserts itself is now being felt in theology, and perhaps it will be specially felt in eschatology. Traditional eschatology seemed to understand the consummation as a kind of escape from the vicissitudes of time, from the "change and decay" that we see in all around, into a realm where nothing would be subject to change any more. "Rest everlasting" was the ideal. At least, this is certainly how it appeared in Christian devotion. *O quanta qualia sunt illa sabbata* . . .

> "O what their joy and their glory must be,
> Those endless sabbaths the blessed ones see!"[1]

To one brought up in Scotland, this seems more like a recipe for *acedia* than for that fullness of life which the consummation is supposed to bring. It suggests a dreary series of rainy Sunday afternoons in Glasgow when pubs and restaurants are closed, football parks are deserted, movie houses are dark: a grey semi-existence, in which absolutely nothing happens.

But before we can go on to talk of eschatology and time, we have to make some distinctions. Those philosophers of recent decades, from Bergson to Heidegger, who have had

---

1. *English Hymnal*, 465.

a special interest in time and temporality, have also distinguished various kinds of time. They make their distinctions differently, but in one way or another they agree in distinguishing what may be called "clock time" or "world time" from the time or temporality of the human existent. Both man and everything else are subject to clock time and calendar time. We are always at a "now," and every such now marks the division between the "no longer" which constitutes the past and the "not yet" which constitutes the future. It is no accident that we use negative expressions, "no longer" and "not yet," for past and future, for according to clock time, it is the now, this instant, that is real. Things, and presumably also animals, are simply "in time," that is to say, they persist from instant to instant. Their past, present, and future are related only externally. Man too is "in time," in the sense that he too must live in this successiveness, and clock time is real for him. Yet although man is *in time,* we also say that he *has time* or *takes time.* Man cannot transcend time, but he can and does transcend the "now" of mere successiveness. He can reach back into the past by memory, and because he is an historical being, this means that not only his own personal past but the past of his community is accessible to him. Moreover, there is a sense in which this past can become present to him. In personal existence, the past affects the present not just through a chain of causes and effects persisting through the intervening "nows," but in a much more direct way, as the past event, made present through memory, discloses possibilities for decision in the present moment. In an analogous fashion, man reaches out into the future through anticipation, prediction, decision. His future too is drawn into the present, so that he does not just remain externally related to it. We can say that man is not only in time; he ex-sists into time, to the extent that he takes time and has time.

Transcendence of the now is essential to authentic or mature personhood, though admittedly other things are essential as well. But it is openness to both past and future that makes possible a realistic assessment of the current situation and a commitment to realistic possibilities in that situation. The most typical case of the immature person is that of the man who lives only from moment to moment, his life dictated by chance circumstances or random desires. Yet equally inauthentic is the case of the man who lives in the past, feeding on memories that are irrelevant to present demands; or the man who has escaped into a future of fantasy and who builds a dream world. The imbalances that are possible for the individual appear too in communities, where they often take the form of a religious faith. There can be a retreat into tradition so that the threatening future is held at bay; or there can be an escape from an intolerable present into the wilder kinds of futuristic apocalyptic. But a full humanity always requires a relatedness to all three of the ways in which man relates to time—the temporal ecstasies of the past, present, and future whereby he ex-sists into the time and is not merely in time.

An attempt to take the notions of time, history, and becoming more seriously in the interpretation of Christian doctrines must have regard to the whole range of man's temporality, that is to say, to both his past and his future as these relate to his present. Christian doctrines have in fact frequently been distorted by an almost exclusive emphasis on one particular dimension of time, usually the past. A good example is the doctrine of the atonement, which has usually been explicated in terms of what God *has done* for men, rather than on what he *is doing* now or *will do* in the future. Of course, such distortions call forth their own corrections in the history of theology, and one can point to instances of this on many occasions in the past. As far as the doctrine of the atonement is concerned, one might mention the work of the Scottish nineteenth-century theologian, John McLeod Campbell, an important part of which was to claim that alongside what he called the "retrospective aspect" of the atonement one must have in view its "prospective aspect," and that the latter even has a certain priority.[2]

2. *The Nature of the Atonement* (London, 1906), pp. 151 ff.

There are some doctrines which, by the very nature of the doctrine itself, might seem to have an inherent reference to a particular dimension of time. Yet, on examination, it will appear that here too an adequate interpretation calls for relating the doctrine to all three of those temporal ecstasies in which man exists. A good example is the doctrine of creation. Almost inevitably, one thinks of the past, of origins, of a beginning *in* time, or even of a beginning *of* time. But contemporary theology is more interested in showing the relation of the doctrine to the present and the future. The notion of an absolute beginning is a very difficult one. Creation is seen rather as a continuing process which is significant for man's understanding of his relations both to God and the world.

Conversely, eschatology seems to be an area of doctrine where the future is of decisive importance. By definition, eschatology deals with "the last things." But the idea of an absolute end is just as difficult as the idea of an absolute beginning. Furthermore, as Paul Tillich argues, when we talk of the *eschaton* in theology, we have in mind more the qualitative than the temporal connotations of the word.[3] In any case, in spite of the direction towards the future that is implicit in the notion of eschatology, this too must be understood like creation as a continuing process or, rather, as a continuing aspect of that history in which man has existed, now exists, and will continue to exist.

Let us now pass in review some of the commoner ways in which eschatology has been interpreted, paying special attention to the question of which particular dimension of temporality has been stressed in each of them. Perhaps the difficulty of arriving at any adequate interpretation acceptable to a modern outlook is the main reason for neglecting eschatology in the theology of our time, though, if we are to believe the New Testament scholars, it was of major importance for the New Testament writers themselves.

The obvious place to begin is with futuristic eschatology. The prototype for this kind of interpretation is to be found

3. *Systematic Theology,* vol. 3 (Chicago, 1963), p. 395.

in the Synoptic Gospels. This is the most dramatic and mythological way of understanding Christian eschatology. The world has come into the last days and the end is imminent. "Truly, I say to you, there are some standing here who will not taste death before they see the kingdom of God come with power."[4] The Son of Man will return on the clouds—or perhaps he will come for the first time, for this is not clear. The kingdom of God will be established, though the Gospels can also speak as if the kingdom were breaking in now. There will be a judgment, and men will be assigned to destinies either of bliss or torment.

Although this imagery is so remote from our modern ways of thinking, I believe that we can still have an idea of the extraordinary power which such eschatological convictions must have exercised in the lives of the people who held them. To believe that one was living in the face of an end that might happen tomorrow, and, in any case, very soon, must have imparted a tremendous sense of urgency, responsibility, and vitality. "The appointed time has grown very short."[5] Surely a partial explanation of the amazing energy of the early Christian community is to be sought in its intense conviction of the approaching end.

But the conviction of the early community turned out to be mistaken. The end did not take place. Scoffers came along, asking: "Where is the promise of his coming? For ever since the fathers fell asleep, all things have continued as they were from the beginning of creation."[6] The end was postponed to the indefinite future. But we must notice that as soon as this happens, eschatology loses most of its power. The tremendous sense of urgency and responsibility and the energy which this sense calls forth depend on the conviction that the time is very short, that the end is almost upon us. When the end is removed to the distant future, it is taken out of existential time and relegated to calendar time, it shares in the negativity of the "not yet" and it be-

---

4. Mk. 9, 2.
5. 1 Cor. 7, 29.
6. 2 Pet. 3, 4.

comes neutralized and ineffective. It might even induce complacency if it becomes the belief that all things are moving inevitably towards some far-off divine event, but the whole business is conceived on such a vast cosmic scale that people feel it has very little to do with them.

Of course, we reject any literal reading of the New Testament imagery. But more than that, I think we reject any purely futuristic eschatology, however refined its concepts might become. I suspect that most people today believe that things will go on much as they have from the beginning of creation. Perhaps they will get better in various ways. Perhaps many limited ends will be achieved. But would we ever arrive at a kingdom of God or an omega point when we could say that God had indeed consummated the work of creation? Would we not immediately look out on some new horizon—and if human existence is through and through temporal and historical, would we not have to do so, or cease to exist? Of course, other kinds of ends may threaten from time to time, and in the face of them men may recapture momentarily something of the sense of living eschatologically. Presumably, there will almost certainly come a time when changes in the sun will make the continuation of human life on this planet impossible; but probably by the time he faces that end, man will have developed the technological means of migrating to another more hospitable part of the universe. Long before that, he may be threatened with an end arising from the misuse of his own power in nuclear warfare, and in our own generation we have already had some sense of the possibility of history's coming to an end. But we should recognize that ends of this kind are entirely different from what the New Testament writers had in mind.

As an alternative to futuristic eschatology, what about the realized eschatology that many New Testament scholars have advocated in the past few decades? Can it help us to reach a more adequate interpretation?

A thoroughgoing realized eschatology puts everything

into the past. The end has already happened. This time the paradigm is St. John's Gospel. The believer has already passed from death to life, and his eternal life is already being actualized. The decisive judgment too has already taken place in the incarnate life of Christ. Some interpreters of the Fourth Gospel argue further that even the return of the Son of Man has already happened, for this is identified with the coming of the Paraclete or Advocate.

No doubt the Fourth Gospel retains traces of a futuristic eschatology, but on the whole the eschatological events have been realized. Scholars differ about the reasons for this transformation of eschatological teaching. Some believe that since the Fourth Gospel comes from near the end of the first century, it was disappointment that the end had not come that led to a radically revised understanding of eschatology, so that one could now assert that the end had indeed come. It can also be argued that it was not disappointment but rather the intense experience of new life and rebirth that led the author of this Gospel to assert that the end had already come and that Christians were living in the new age.

But however one accounts for this realized eschatology, it still presents us with many problems, especially when we try to relate it to our own situation today. Perhaps the early generations of Christians could really think of themselves as living in a new age. Even as late as the beginning of the fourth century, we find St. Athanasius pointing to the renewal and cleansing of society as a kind of empirical evidence of the truth of Christianity.[7]

But what are we going to say, living among the ambiguities of the twentieth century many centuries after these events of resurrection, judgment, coming of the Spirit, and the like? I think we must frankly say that if that was the end and this is the new age, and if it has all happened, then it does not seem to amount to very much. If eschatology has been realized, well, it is rather a damp squib.

7. *De Incarnatione*, 51–53.

A third possibility of interpretation is the demythologized eschatology of Bultmann. Although it has something in common with a realized eschatology and is specially oriented to the Fourth Gospel, Bultmann's account of the matter tries to bring eschatology into the present, into the here and now of our actual existence. Every moment is potentially an eschatological moment, so that eschatology is neither something that will happen nor something that has happened, but something that keeps on happening whenever, to use Bultmann's words, "Christ is born, suffers, dies, and is raised up to eternal life" in the soul of a Christian believer.[8] Every man lives in the face of an imminent end, namely, his own death, so that we all understand what it means to live eschatologically. But it is in this situation of being delivered over to sin and death that man hears the kerygma which summons him to share in the death and resurrection of Christ. All the eschatological ideas, in this interpretation, become symbols of present realities. Judgment is present, for the hearer is placed under the judgment of the kerygma. Heaven is present, for what is heaven but the fuller risen life which the Christian shares in the body of Christ? The alternative of hell is a present possibility too, for what is hell but the disintegration and eventual break-up of an existence that is alienated by sin?

There is very much that is persuasive in Bultmann's demythologized eschatology—indeed, I doubt if any other contemporary scholar has been nearly so successful in showing that eschatology need not be dismissed as just an ancient superstition and that its imagery conceals truths that apply very pointedly to man's situation today.

Nevertheless, I think that Bultmann's interpretation of eschatology is open to two objections. The first and most obvious is its individualism. Eschatology, in Bultmann, is not only realized and demythologized but also individualized. The locus of the eschatological event is placed in the soul of the individual believer as he responds in faith to the kerygma. In this respect, Bultmann remains in the tradition

8. *The Presence of Eternity* (New York, 1957), p. 153.

of pietism. His eschatology has to do with the destiny of the single human existent, not with the community of faith and still less with creation as a whole. Bultmann has been justly criticized both for the inadequacy of his doctrine of the church or community of faith, and for his failure to develop any social theology or to provide any foundation for such a social theology. The other objection to Bultmann's demythologized eschatology is his almost complete excision of any future reference from his interpretation. One could base this objection on the fact that the future aspect of eschatology is so prominent in most of the New Testament writings that any alleged interpretation which simply omitted it would hardly be a valid interpretation. However, the objection that is more relevant to this essay is concerned with our earlier contention that the interpretation of Christian doctrine generally—if this is to be done in a way that takes seriously the temporal constitution of a man, in whom, after all, the event of faith takes place—must have regard to all the temporal ecstasies of human existence. To omit any one of them is to give a less than adequate and possibly a distorted interpretation. I do not say that Bultmann altogether omits the future reference, for he frequently speaks of the Christian life as the receiving of a capacity to meet the future in love, and by the "transcendence" of God he seems sometimes to understand that God is always before us. But these references to the future are set within the context of individual existence. A future of history and, even more, a cosmic future are matters which Bultmann leaves aside. He considers them speculative and objectifying. In the language that we have used earlier in this essay, such speculations would move our understanding of Christian faith from existential time into calendar time.

Perhaps there just is no way of combining the existential-individual type of eschatology found in Bultmann with the notions of an end in history or in the cosmic process. It may be that here we have two hermeneutic approaches that cannot be brought together. Yet some kind of synthesis has to be attempted, or else we seem to be left with an inadequate and one-sided eschatology.

It is at this point that it may be useful to turn to the views of Jürgen Moltmann. At first sight, Moltmann seems to supply those dimensions of an eschatological doctrine that are lacking in Bultmann. He offers a social interpretation as against Bultmann's individualism, and his future-oriented eschatology contrasts with Bultmann's preoccupation with the present. Furthermore, there are strong existential elements in Moltmann's thought, and the fact that his understanding of the end is in historical terms, rather than in the cosmic terms of someone like Teilhard de Chardin, might indicate that his views do not involve us in that kind of objectification to which Bultmann so strongly objects.

Yet when we bring the views of Bultmann and Moltmann into confrontation with each other, it soon becomes clear that there are some important points where they remain incompatible. If Moltmann on his side has the advantage of a broader, socially significant interpretation of eschatology, Bultmann has on his side a more consistent method of interpretation, and one that, as it seems to me, is more respectful towards the contemporary scientific and secular outlook.

The major point of dispute concerns the interpretation of the resurrection of Christ. Let us notice first that Bultmann and Moltmann are in agreement that the resurrection is not to be separated from the crucifixion. But from there on, they diverge. According to Bultmann, "faith in the resurrection is really the same thing as faith in the saving efficacy of the cross."[9] He is quite clear that the resurrection in itself cannot be considered as an historical event. It was indeed a reality, but a reality as faith in the cross and as a self-understanding among the disciples. But Moltmann is dissatisfied with this account. He thinks that the resurrection is an historical reality and that there was in some sense a real resurrection of Jesus as a prior condition of the resurrection faith in the disciples. He makes the forthright claim

9. *Kerygma and Myth*, p. 41.

that "Christianity stands or falls with the reality of the raising of Jesus from the dead by God."[10]

Immediately we come up against the vexed question of what we mean by an historical event. It seems fairly clear that the church would never have come into existence unless there had been among the earliest disciples a profound conviction that Jesus was risen from the dead. The appearance of this belief is undoubtedly an historical event, and one that can be investigated. But what of the content of the belief, the supposed raising of Jesus from the dead by God? It seems to me that to answer the question of whether this content can be considered as an historical event, we have to consider the canons of the secular historian, and we have to abide by them. Several years ago, Helmut Thielicke rightly saw that Bultmann's exclusion of the resurrection from the category of historical events depended on his implicit acceptance of the tests by which the secular historian distinguishes historical report from legend and myth, and especially the three principles laid down by Ernst Troeltsch —causality, analogy, and immanence.[11] As against this, Thielicke argued that the Christian theologian ought to take the decisive events of the New Testament as supplying the concept of what history, in the authentic sense, really is. I do not myself think that this is a reasonable proposal, and it seems specially inapposite at a time when the Christian church is committed to taking with a new seriousness the integrity of the so-called "secular" disciplines. It would surely be a strange reversal to triumphalism if the theologian were to lay down to the historian the criteria for his research.

Moltmann has a much more careful and complex approach to the problem than Thielicke, and he shows himself more respectful to the methods of the historian. Yet I believe that he gets into grave logical difficulties, and that these render very questionable a central part of his argument.

10. *Theology of Hope* (New York and Evanston, 1967), p. 165.
11. *The Expository Times,* 67:6 (March 1956), p. 176.

We have seen already that he takes the resurrection of Jesus Christ to have been, in some sense, a real historical event, the content of which is not exhausted in terms of the awakening of a new self-understanding in the disciples. But Moltmann is willing to concede that, in order to believe in such an event, it is reasonable to look for analogous events. However, we are told that up till now there is no analogy. The resurrection is said to be an event "without parallel." There are no resurrections going on now that would verify the possibility of such events, and confirm our faith in the resurrection of Christ. The analogy lies in what is still to come.[12] There will be a resurrection of the dead, and this will provide the eschatological verification of the resurrection of Christ.

The logical difficulties of this situation are fairly obvious. It is claimed that there has been a resurrection, and on the basis of this we hope for a resurrection of the dead in the future. Yet, on the other hand, it will only be the actualization of this eschatological resurrection that will verify the claim that Jesus rose from the dead. There has been resurrection, and there will be resurrection, but I find it very hard to see how one can believe in past or future resurrections without some present analogous happening. Surely when the historian looks for an analogy to a reported historical event, this analogy must lie within accessible experience, or it can have no value. Past and future cannot be used to verify each other without reference to the present, especially when we remember the universal tendency to idealize both past and future. We may recall that Alice in Wonderland inquired if she might have some jam. She was told that there was jam yesterday and there will be jam tomorrow, but there is no jam today. And unfortunately it always is today.

"Epiphany" is a bad word in Moltmann's *Theology of Hope*. An entire tradition of Christian thought that has centered on the sense of God's presence is dismissed. But with me, "epiphany" is a good word. If there were no

12. *Op. cit.*, p. 180.

present epiphanies of God amid the ambiguities of the world, how could we have any beliefs about his action in past or future? We need presence as well as promise.

One might compare with Moltmann's argument the reasoning put forward in a recent book by F. H. Cleobury. He too argues that belief in the resurrection of Christ would be confirmed by analogous events, and he claims that we do in fact have instances of something similar to the appearances of the risen Lord in the cases reported by psychical researchers.[13] The force of Cleobury's claim depends, of course, on the extent to which one is prepared to acknowledge the reliability of psychical research. However, because the analogies to which he points are accessible in the present and are capable, at least in principle, of verification or falsification, one has to admit that his argument is more empirical and logically sounder than one which appeals to verification "at the end."

Bultmann too argues that there is resurrection now, and that it is because we can experience such renewal that we believe in the resurrection of Christ; or, rather, that our present experience of renewal is itself the meaning of faith in the resurrection. But this takes us back into the individualistic and rather subjective kind of eschatological interpretation, and we have already acknowledged it to be inadequate.

Our results so far are somewhat negative. Is there any way at all of understanding eschatology, such as would preserve the existential dimension stressed by Bultmann and yet might allow us to develop the futural and social aspects of eschatology that we find in Moltmann—and perhaps even the cosmic aspect, on which Teilhard de Chardin has concentrated attention?

I suggest that the notion of "eternal life" may turn out to be the most useful concept for integrating the various aspects of eschatology. I should say that I am not trying to offer an exegesis of the New Testament idea of eternal life. I hope that my interpretation will be not unrelated to the

13. *A Return to Natural Theology* (London, 1967), p. 204.

New Testament, but its primary orientation is philosophical.

More than any other concept, the notion of eternal life can gather up and relate some of the loose ends that tend to accumulate when we deal with the different styles of eschatological interpretation—realized, demythologized, future, existential, individual, historical, cosmic, and so on. Our earlier remarks have made it clear that eternal life has nothing to do with the idea of an eternity that is timeless or opposed to time. It is a question of transcending the "now," the passing instant, but not of transcending time as such. Eternal life is the development to the limit of that natural tendency of the human existent to take time and have time rather than just to be in time, and this happens as he extends himself into his past and future, and relates them to his present. As an existent, man already has, shall we say, a "taste" of eternal life and the sense of a destiny that goes beyond mere transience. An attempt has been made recently by Wolfhart Pannenberg to show how the analysis of man's being points to his fulfillment in a mode of existence that rises above death,[14] and of course this line of argument is one that has many precedents in the history both of philosophy and of theology.

Furthermore, just because eternal life tends to draw the individual beyond the borders of his single existence, it is a concept which enables us to move from individualistic ways of thinking about eschatology to more communal and historical ways. The past, present, and future to which the single human existent relates himself are not merely his own —they merge into the past, present, and future of his community. He is part of a larger social whole, and his own private story merges into a history, providing a wider context within which his life is set. The historical community too has its memory and likewise its anticipation, so that we can think of it as constituted by temporality and related to time in ways that are analogous to what holds in the case of the single individual. Indeed, we might even ask whether, as the Hegelian philosophers used to teach, the community

14. *Grundzüge der Christologie* (Gütersloh, 1964), pp. 79–82.

is not more properly called an "individual" than the single existent. For individuality implies a measure of wholeness and completeness, and this belongs to the social reality rather than to the single existent who, apart from his social context, is a fragmented abstraction. It is true that the Hegelians usually identified this larger communal individual with the state. Perhaps the Christian should identify it with the church—the church understood not as a separate community, but as ideally the focus of the whole human race. There can be no salvation for the individual apart from the social reality to which he belongs.

But an eschatological faith must look beyond even this historico-social whole to a still larger unity—the gathering up of all things in God. Again, it is the notion of eternal life that might give us some clue as to how this might happen. May we suppose that God too takes time and has time for the work of creation, and that just as we transcend the instant and gather together our past, present, and future, so on a much vaster scale and in a more complete manner, God gathers into a unity the past, present, and future of the cosmos. We need not suppose that this is a process that would ever be finished—rather, it would seem likely that every *eschaton* or omega point would open the horizon on a new one.

It is clear that such speculations carry us far beyond what can be known with any certitude. Yet it would seem that if we live with real hope for the world and if we are to work for its future with some confidence that what we are doing is worthwhile, we are committed to some kind of speculative eschatology. As Moltmann puts it, "the transforming mission requires in practice a certain *Weltanschauung,* a confidence in the world and a hope for the world."[15] Hope, after all, would not be hope if it were based on infallible calculation. Neither should it be confused with optimism. Hope, like faith, is a risk that we take as finite existents, and perhaps we can hardly help taking it.

15. *Op. cit.,* p. 288.

SECULARISM, RESPONSIBLE BELIEF, AND THE "THEOLOGY OF HOPE"

Van A. Harvey

I

There is one old problem in particular that continues to haunt me, although it is always assuming new and fascinating forms. In its most general and rough form, one might say that it is the problem of the truth of Christian belief. More specifically, it has to do with the problem of believing responsibly in the modern world. I am troubled by the massive presence of doubt among us and by the fact that this doubt in many souls is frequently infused by a fierce sense of intellectual integrity. I am concerned, in short, about the collision between a certain moral policy of judgment and Christian believing, a collision that makes it possible for many to regard the believing and hoping of Christians as being irresponsible. My concern probably reflects the old-fashioned view that a theology or philosophy cannot long survive or recommend itself to men unless it seems to them to be true, which is to say, unless it seems to provide some viable way of symbolizing and articulating elements in their own experience.

It has been argued that one of the virtues of the "theology

of hope" is that it shows that the question of belief is now irrelevant, at least in the way it has most often been posed. The problem of belief, it is said, has traditionally been associated with the question, "What can I know?" But this question necessarily throws the weight on such categories of evidence, mind, present reality, being, *logos,* and has led Western Christendom inevitably to the crisis of unbelief in which it now stands. The more important question is, "For what can I hope?", and it is to this question that Christianity speaks. It says that men can hope for the resurrection of the dead, and it is this hope that leads to revolutionary action in the world.

There is a measure of—what can one say but—truth in this reply. Still, two things may be said about it. The first is in the form of a question. Can one so easily play hoping off against believing? Is it even possible to give any content to a hope apart from our beliefs about the past and the present? If we hope for the resurrection of the dead, this hope, surely, is grounded in a claim about a past event and what that event allegedly discloses about a presently existing divine power whose mode of being, therefore, cannot be entirely future. And if we cannot hope for such a resurrection, that, too, is rooted in a dubiety about the past. Our hoping or not hoping is itself very closely connected with our believing or disbelieving.

The second thing to say is that our discussion has, at the outset, been launched at too high a level of abstraction. The words "truth" and "belief" are just too rough-hewn for any precise discussion of the issue, just as the simple word "hope" is also singularly useless. Our modernity consists, in part, in the fact that we now see that there is no one problem of truth as such, just as there is no single answer that can be given to the question, "What can I know?" The so-called problem of truth, however profound it sounds in introductory philosophy textbooks, is an umbrella-like phrase under which far too many different kinds of questions lose their distinctive shadows.

To say something is true, quite generally, is at least to say that it is worthy of being believed. But what makes any particular claim worthy of being believed depends on the data and warrants that are brought forward in support of it. What data and warrants are relevant for justifying the claim will depend on the logical type of claim it is, on what logical field it belongs to.[1] The kinds of data and warrants brought forward to justify a claim about a political candidate's chances of being nominated for the Presidency of the United States will necessarily differ from the kinds of data appealed to in justification of a claim about the authenticity of an ancient manuscript, or about the correlation between changes in temperature and the behavior of a certain gas, or about the effectiveness of fluoridation in preventing dental decay, or about the degree to which the Industrial Revolution was a function of slavery. What constitutes the standard for worthiness of belief will vary from field to field and no single standard can be stretched to cover all the kinds of claims men make in scientific journals, courts of law, history books, newspapers, literary magazines, mathematics textbooks, and psychiatric offices.

When one looks at the matter in this fashion, one can see how misleading it is even to talk about the truth of the Christian faith, for it is clear that the Christian faith is made up of a number of logically diverse though related strands of belief. It contains anthropological, ontological, historical, theological, valuational, and interpretative beliefs, all of which are subtly woven together to form the closely knit garment of belief called the Christian faith.

To talk about truth and Christian faith in this fashion already reveals how deeply we have been influenced by one aspect of the modern secular spirit, its commitment to the specialization of knowledge. The institutional embodiment of this is, of course, the modern university. The university does not recognize experts in truth in general but

1. See Stephen Toulmin, *The Uses of Argument* (New York, 1958), chap. 1.

only biologists, physicists, historians, anthropologists, political scientists, and the like. There is no universal method of acquiring truth or assessing claims. There are only particular methods suited to particular and delimited types of inquiry.

In any discussion of the problem of belief in the modern world, it is necessary to stay in close touch with this aspect of secularism; otherwise, it will be impossible to understand exactly what the modern problem is, how it arises, and what can be done about it. One of the greatest defects of the "theology of hope" is, as I shall try to show, that it does not sufficiently grasp the problem, and so the solution it offers is unsatisfactory. I am aware, of course, that the term "secularism" has become a large category-bin into which authors tend to throw all of their miscellaneous and loosely drawn file cards. Secularism is a very complex phenomenon, and I do not propose to try to define or describe it. It is sufficient for my purposes to concentrate on two closely related though distinct aspects of secularism that impinge directly on theology and with which it must deal. The first is what I shall call the ethics of belief that informs the intellectual elite of secular culture. The second is the pluralization of religious belief that confronts common men and intellectuals alike. I will discuss the implications of this ethics of belief for the "theology of hope" in the next portion of this essay and, following that, I will turn to the significance of religious pluralization for the "theology of hope" in particular and theology in general.

II

Any sensitive reader of philosophic and religious literature since the Enlightenment cannot fail to observe that the rejection of Christian belief is often infused by a passionate moral indignation. This indignation is most often directed at the content of specific religious doctrines that strike the critic as morally reprehensible, such as the doctrines of hell and predestination. But occasionally, the indignation is directed not so much at the content of a doctrine as it is at the very act of believing itself.[2] The critic is morally outraged because the very act of believing, he feels, manifests and fosters credulity and obscurantism. One of the most powerful of these critics of believing was W. K. Clifford, the Cambridge scientist, who was the first, so far as I am aware, to use the phrase the "ethics of belief." Clifford argued that "it is wrong, always, everywhere, and for anyone, to believe anything on insufficient evidence."[3]

This statement is unintelligible apart from the almost Faustian will-to-truth which has infused Western culture since Socrates. But this will-to-truth did not truly become revolutionary until after the Enlightenment, when it became attached to specific types of inquiry such as astronomy, physics, history, anthropology, biology, and psychology. The result was not only an explosion in knowledge but the gradual emergence of a new cultural ideal of responsible judgment, a new morality of knowledge.

This ideal inevitably found concrete expression in the educational policy informing the schools and universities, those institutions which more than any other have shaped the development of Western secular culture. The underlying assumption of this ideal is that credulity is a great vice from which men need to be liberated and that credulity can only be eradicated by the systematic inculcation of the virtues of independence of mind, skepticism towards unfounded claims, and the habit of seeking out all the evidence

2. Some philosophers argue that it is misleading to speak of believing as a voluntary act and, hence, as subject to moral appraisal. It follows that they also believe that it is misleading to speak of an ethics of belief. See C. K. Grant, *Belief and Action* (Durham, N.C., 1960); and H. H. Price, "Belief and Will" in *Aristotelean Society Supplementary Volume*, XXVIII (1954), pp. 1–26. I have sought to meet this argument in an article, "Is There an Ethics of Belief?" in a forthcoming issue of *The Journal of Religion*.

3. "The Ethics of Belief," in Walter Kaufmann, *Religion from Tolstoy to Camus* (New York and Evanston, 1961), p. 206.

relevant to the truth and falsity of a claim before assenting to it. As the historian G. M. Young has colorfully expressed it, a student should be taught that he has no more right to an opinion for which he cannot account than for a pint of beer for which he cannot pay.[4] This educational policy dictates that schools should drill into the minds of the young that a reasonable man in any field of inquiry can be recognized by the care with which he formulates his judgments so that they might be understood and rationally assessed. Moreover, he will invariably qualify his judgments and so indicate the degree of assurance he thinks properly attaches to them. His arguments, whether before courts of law or in newspapers or in classrooms, will be liberally sprinkled with the judicious qualification, which is the sure sign of the discriminating mind at work. The reasonable man does not traffic in mere claims but in carefully modified claims.

The difficulty with W. K. Clifford's position is that the category of belief, as he uses it, is too broad, and the appeal to sufficient evidence is unexamined. We are now more aware than he was of the various logical types of belief and how misleading is the simple appeal to sufficient evidence. What would it mean, for example, to demand evidence for the moral belief that one ought not to believe anything on insufficient evidence? One might ask for evidence for a factual belief but not for a moral belief. Moreover, among the various kinds of belief about facts, the standards of sufficient evidence and argument vary greatly. Finally, the ethic Clifford advocates seems impractical because of the great weight he puts upon skepticism.[5] We necessarily acquire countless beliefs from our infancy, all more or less on authority. Is there a specific date—say our twenty-first birthday—at which we should take a sabbatical and laboriously evaluate every single belief we hold in order to establish whether it is justified by the evidence?

4. *Victorian Essays* (London, 1962), p. 7.
5. See Michael Polanyi's critique of this ethic in *Personal Knowledge* (New York and Evanston, 1958), chap. IX.

Nevertheless, it would be too cheap a victory to dismiss the problem of responsible belief by disposing of Clifford's formulation of it. We might, for example, distinguish broadly between evidential and non-evidential beliefs and argue that there are standards for each by which we can judge whether they are held responsibly or not.[6] Or we might approach the problem by linking kinds of beliefs with professional spheres of responsibility. We might say that certain roles in life require a self-consciousness about and responsibility for areas of belief that do not accrue to other roles. Suppose, to illustrate, you are a judge and that you and your colleagues hold yourselves responsible for being informed concerning the previous decisions of courts on the matter before your bench. Suppose also that you hold some proposition *p* about a previous decision to be true. Suppose, finally, that someone points out to you that *p* is false and provides you evidence in support of this. Were you to ignore the evidence and to persist in your belief, it would not be unintelligible if your peers were to form the judgment that your believing *p* was irresponsible.

It is important to emphasize that this ideal of responsible judgment is not simply "out there" in secular culture in contrast to some different ideal "in here" in the church. The new morality of knowledge is also a part of the mental furniture of many Christians. Christians who are judges, historians, newspaper correspondents, and scientists also judge one another and themselves in terms of independence of mind, rigorous assessment of evidence and argument, and, above all, balanced judgment. Indeed, it is only because this ideal of judgment penetrated the church that biblical criticism within the community of faith became an actuality. We take this ethic so much for granted that we scarcely realize the magnitude of the revolution in consciousness involved. For centuries, the church regarded skepticism and doubt concerning certain historical claims

6. See Ralph Barton Perry, *In the Spirit of William James* (Bloomington, Ind., 1958), pp. 170–208.

to be a sin while credulity was regarded as a virtue. The revolution in consciousness did not come about because the church suddenly discovered the will-to-truth. In a sense, the church always had this. Rather, the revolution came about when the church was forced to respect the autonomy of the special empirical disciplines, which is to say, when the church realized that to claim a proposition about our experience to be true is something like claiming a right to a title. Both have to be justified, and the justification of truth claims is relative to specific methods of inquiry and standards of assessment. The world taught the church that the latter had no special competence in judgments concerning human experience, especially history. The more liberal biblical critic did not refute the sometimes ingenious arguments of conservative churchmen trying to retain the hegemony of faith over biblical inquiry. The latter were simply by-passed. They were not appointed to the academic posts in the universities because they would not enter the academic arena with its underlying rules which reflected the new ethics of belief.

It is only against this background that we can understand the pathos of that doubt which afflicts not only many secular men but many Christian theologians as well. This doubt is often compounded with a sense of moral integrity. Indeed, the nineteenth and twentieth centuries have seen the rise of a new phenomenon within the church, the alienated theologian, one who has felt morally compelled to relinquish certain traditional Christian beliefs because he can, in conscience, no longer hold them. No church can afford to ignore this phenomenon: someone who out of love for the truth decides that the church does not represent that truth.

It is very important at this point, however, that we not generalize about doubt or belief, because it is just the large generalization that will lead us astray. The problem of integrity properly arises when a given religious belief seems to conflict with some specialized form of inquiry and its results. Sophisticated secular men and alienated theologians are aware that no problem of integrity arises if the religious belief in question could not in the nature of the case conflict with some delimited intellectual discipline. If these men do not believe, say, in the existence of God, and are aware that this belief is such as not to involve a conflict with some specialized sphere of knowledge, their disbelief is not primarily a matter of integrity in the way that disbelieving in the creation of the world in six days, or in the Mosaic authorship of the Pentateuch, or in the historical accuracy of the picture of Jesus in the Fourth Gospel, is a matter of integrity. Integrity is at stake when a contingent claim requires a belief that necessarily involves a collision with the methods of a specific field of inquiry.

It is precisely at this point that biblical criticism, particularly, and historical inquiry, generally, pose the problem for so many. The problem is not, as Tillich and Bultmann have tended to argue, that Christian faith cannot be dependent on the uncertainties of historical knowledge. It is, rather, that faith seems to require *a degree of certitude* with respect to certain historical claims that does not seem justified. Perhaps it does not seem justified because these claims are disputed by New Testament scholars themselves and there seems no way for a layman to resolve the dispute except arbitrarily. Or perhaps it does not seem justified because the degree of certitude seems incommensurate with the strength of the evidence and the arguments brought forward on behalf of the claim. Or perhaps the claim seems incompatible with some area of present knowledge against the background of which we make our judgments about the past.

It could be argued that the history of modern Protestant theology is the history of a series of salvage operations, that is, attempts to reconcile the Christian faith with the ethic of critical judgment.[7] Protestant liberalism, dialectical theology, the new quest, the new hermeneutic, the Pannenberg

7. See my *The Historian and the Believer* (New York, 1966).

school, process theology are all efforts to deal with the problem of intellectual integrity by turning aside the criticism that one can only be a Christian believer at the price of sacrificing the standards of intellectual honesty that dominate the consciousness of the Western intellectual.

Moltmann's theology may also be interpreted as one of these salvage operations, and one reason this theology appeals to many, I suspect, is that it seems to resolve what is loosely called the faith-history problem. It seems to offer a way of doing justice to God's promise in Jesus Christ, on the one hand, without requiring a sacrifice of the intellect, on the other. We can see how Moltmann's theology serves this interest if we focus on his interpretation of the resurrection of Jesus. In its essentials, his view looks roughly like this. The biblical view of revelation is not that Jesus was the epiphany of some eternally present metaphysical reality. Rather, the essence of God is his faithfulness, which will only be fully manifested in his quickening of the dead. The logic of faith, Moltmann thinks, can be discerned in the writings of Paul. Because God has the power to quicken the dead, the fulfillment of God's promise is possible, and because God has raised Christ from the dead, the fulfillment of the promise is certain.[8] Thus one can say that Christian faith stands or falls with the raising of Jesus from the dead by God.[9] In the resurrection, faith discerns the promise of a totality of new being,[10] and it is in this hope that the Christian is able to bear the sorrows of the world.

When the argument is put so baldly, it throws into relief the close connection between believing and hoping in Moltmann's view. The past and the future hang together. But it is just because they do hang together that the "theology of hope" is confronted by the problems raised by historical inquiry. How is it possible for a critical mind to give a firm

8. *Theology of Hope* (New York and Evanston, 1967), p. 145; cf. pp. 194, 200 ff.
9. *Ibid.*, p. 165.
10. *Ibid.*, p. 196.

assent to the historical judgment that Jesus was raised from the dead without violating the standards of responsible historical judgment? Moltmann is quite aware of the problem, and he makes a philosophical move at this point which is now almost standard in some Christian apologetic circles. He argues that critical historical inquiry only poses a problem of honesty if one assumes that the critical historian is in fact capable of assessing the truth of the resurrection belief.[11] But he is not, because historical inquiry as it has been practiced since the Enlightenment is based upon anthropocentric, pantheistic, and atheistic presuppositions that determine in advance a negative judgment with respect to the resurrection.[12] The modern historian simply comes to the texts with an alien understanding of history. His understanding is based, as Ernst Troeltsch saw, on the omnipotence of the principle of analogy. It is on the basis of analogies between past events of the same kind that the historian is enabled "to ascribe probability to them and to interpret aspects of the one on the basis of the known aspects of the other."[13] But this principle, Moltmann argues, necessarily presupposes that all events have a common core of similarity and, therefore, rests on a metaphysics which "sees all historical things in terms of substance."[14] Such a view of history not only precludes the possibility of resurrections, it also destroys the possibility of any truly historical understanding of the genuinely new and unique by making it "only accidental."[15]

Moltmann argues that it follows that if one accepts a view of history based on analogy then one must also concede that the resurrection is not historical.[16] The resurrec-

11. *Ibid.*, pp. 172–182.
12. *Ibid.*, pp. 174, 177.
13. Troeltsch as quoted by Moltmann, *ibid.*, p. 175.
14. *Ibid.*, p. 176.
15. *Ibid.*
16. In Moltmann's Ingersoll Lecture, "Resurrection As Hope," *Harvard Theological Review*, 61:2 (April 1968), 136, he writes that the something which happened to the dead Jesus and the disciples escapes

tion will necessarily elude historical verification because there are no analogies to it. In the face of the resurrection, the historical question not only reaches its objective but its categorical limit.[17] This, however, poses the more radical question whether the modern view of history is an adequate one. Perhaps its inability to deal with the resurrection recoils on the modern historian and calls into question his experience of history.[18]

What, we might ask, are the alternatives to the modern view of history? Moltmann suggests that there are three.[19] First, one could, like Bultmann, abandon history to pantheism and concentrate on the non-objectifiable experience of existential decision. The objection to this, however, is that it leaves the resurrection hanging in the air. Secondly, one could, like Pannenberg, try to develop a concept of history as a whole and concentrate on the dissimilar, the new, and the unique. But this view, Moltmann objects, not only ends up "by losing the feeling for history altogether" but, more importantly, it is theologically inadequate because it fails to see that "the resurrection of Christ does not mean a possibility within the world and its history, but a new possibility altogether for the world, for existence and for history."[20] In short, the resurrection points to the freedom of God to create *ex nihilo*. Finally, and this is Moltmann's own proposal, one could "expose the profound irrationality of the rational cosmos of the modern, technico-scientific world" on which modern secular historical inquiry rests.[21] But this task can only be accomplished by arriving at a new understanding of history and of the possibilities that attach to it when one *presupposes* the raising of Christ

---

historical verification, and that "we must therefore state that the act of the raising of Jesus is not a historically observable and ascertainable event." Cf. *Theology of Hope*, p. 188.

17. See Moltmann's Ingersoll Lecture, *ibid.*
18. *Theology of Hope*, p. 175.
19. *Ibid.*, pp. 177 ff.
20. *Ibid.*, pp. 178 f.
21. *Ibid.*, p. 179.

from the dead.[22] Such a new understanding will be genuinely revolutionary because it turns all of our so-called real experience into an experience that is provisional. "It must therefore contradict all rigid substantio-metaphysical definitions of the common core of similarity in world events, and therefore also the corresponding historical understanding that works with analogy."[23]

What can one say about this radical and iconoclastic proposal for a new method of historical inquiry? The first and most important thing to observe is the rather crude way, philosophically speaking, in which Moltmann identifies modern historical reasoning with analogical reasoning and then identifies this with a rigid metaphysics of substance. Presumably only an outdated and rigid metaphysics of substance has difficulties with the resurrection. This argument, I fear, will not convince many who examine it carefully, and those who have any acquaintance with the recent literature on the philosophy of history will only find it painful reading. Once again, the difficulty arises when we permit ourselves to be mesmerized by the gross generalization and abstraction.

Roughly speaking, it is true that every historian approaches his work with certain assumptions and presuppositions. But these presuppositions are of many different kinds and function at many different levels. Moreover, there is often no neat correlation between these presuppositions and the historian's concrete judgments. Historians are often better (and also worse!) than their presuppositions. The important thing, however, is to take great pains to sort out these various assumptions and to describe precisely how they in fact do function in the historian's inquiry. Unfortunately, the principle of analogy is singularly useless in this respect. We can see this if we observe that the historian, in the nature of the case, makes his judgments, and assesses those of his colleagues, against the background

22. *Ibid.*, p. 180.
23. *Ibid.*

of what I shall loosely call present knowledge. The designation is loose just because present knowledge includes an incredible diversity of types of knowledge and belief. It includes the many sciences as well as types of knowledge that are not the province of any exact science. Present knowledge, we might say, is field-encompassing. Consider, for example, the diversity of scientific knowledge which historians presuppose in their work. The historian presupposes what we might call the laws of ballistics when he assesses the relative capabilities of rifled and smooth-bored artillery at the Battle of Gettysburg and how this dictated strategy and tactics. He takes for granted the science of electronics when he explains how radar made a decisive difference in the Battle for Britain. He assumes the laws of astronomy when he evaluates a report that the sun stood still in the midst of a battle. He presupposes the principles of physiology—the relation between lungs, brain, nerve endings, and vocal chords—when he declares it to be a legend that a saint picked up his head after his execution, placed it under his arm, marched into the cathedral and sang the *Te Deum*. He presupposes meteorology when he doubts the medieval report that blood rained from heaven. Indeed, if the historian did not presuppose this present knowledge, it would be impossible to account for the categories of myth and legend which are so indispensable to historical inquiry.

It is misleading, however, to discuss the problem of presuppositions as if the present knowledge of the historian was primarily scientific in content. The historian also presupposes a great deal of less easily classifiable knowledge and belief. Some of it exists at a relatively high degree of generalization—the relationship between economic class and ideology in Western society, the function of magic and myth in so-called primitive societies—and some of it is quite context-bound—the role of the mercantile classes in the Industrial Revolution, Victorian attitudes towards sex in the middle of the nineteenth century, etc. A great deal of this knowledge cannot be regarded as scientific in any precise sense, but it would be foolish to assume that the warrants or assumptions the historian derives from these bodies of knowledge are equally arbitrary or provisional. These various fields yield generalizations and principles of varying degrees of certainty. There is, for example, much less room for doubt in dating an ancient manuscript by the carbon 14 test than there is when relying on stylistic arguments. So, too, there is much more room for debate with respect to the causes of the Civil War than there is that the Book of Mormon was revealed in its present state to Joseph Smith.

This field-encompassing nature of present knowledge helps illumine why it is true but philosophically misleading to note that "every historian has his presuppositions" as if these presuppositions were all equally faith-like and lacking in justification. This is also why it is useless to note that the historian depends on analogies. In some of these fields, the so-called principle of analogy is so formal a principle as to be of no help at all. And it is certainly false to say that the historian who argues against the background of present knowledge necessarily assumes the fundamental similarity of all events, whatever that means, or is committed to a metaphysics of substance. Process philosophers, linguistic analysts, phenomenologists, existentialists, absolute idealists, all could easily agree that the turning of water into wine is probably legend, that Mary and Joseph probably did not take Jesus down into Egypt, and that the raising of Lazarus is probably a post-resurrection story. Nor does any such process of historical judgment as I have described dictate that every genuinely unique event is to be regarded as merely accidental. It is precisely the modern historian who has taught us to be dubious about the use of analogies and, on the whole, he avoids them like the plague. So, too, he has taught us that it is anachronistic to think that people of ancient times thought and behaved as we think and behave. Indeed, in the case of the New Testament authors, it is just because we know that they were sons of their time and did not have the same standards of probability that we have that we find it difficult to accept as true their stories of the casting out of the demons, the turning of water into wine, the walking on water, and the raising of the dead.

Keeping this field-encompassing nature of history before us, then, let us ask what it could possibly mean for Moltmann to advocate an historical method which "exposes the profound irrationality of the rational cosmos" or that makes all of our real experience provisional. How would such an historical inquiry actually differ from what we now call historical inquiry? What would it mean in the concrete processes of judgment and assessment to consider our knowledge about ballistics, astronomy, physiology, and meteorology provisional? What does Moltmann actually propose with his attack upon the rational cosmos? Does he mean that we will once again seriously entertain reports of snakes talking, axe-heads floating, men walking on water, seas being parted upon command, and men rising up into heaven? The problem is not, I think, whether the cosmos is rational or not but how we go about assessing and giving various degrees of assent to certain concrete claims.

There is a sense in which the critical historian does realize that all of our experience is provisional. He knows, through the processes of studying history itself, that every historian is a child of his time in certain respects, that many of the beliefs he now holds will be seen by later historians to have been relative and time-bound. This is one of the reasons why history must be rewritten in every generation. But the conclusion to draw from this relativity is not that the historian can simply ignore what I have called present knowledge. On the contrary, it could be argued that he is responsible for it, and he exercises this responsibility by accepting what he regards as the best-informed opinion and consensus in any field unless he has compelling reasons of the same logical type for not doing so. No progress in knowledge in any field is possible unless the judgments in that field are rejected for reasons that are themselves rationally assessable. The modern historian knows that what provisional knowledge we have was gained only by those who were loyal to the standards and methods of specific communities of inquiry.

It is important to keep our eye on the function of present knowledge in justifying historical claims, for to make a claim is, as I have said, to imply that it is worthy of being believed. To say that a certain claim is probable or possible is not so much to settle an argument dogmatically; it functions, rather, to alter and make clear the dynamics of historical argument, to shift and localize the burden of proof. When someone claims that a unique event occurred which seems unlikely or incompatible with a specific field of knowledge, to say that it is improbable is to say that the one who makes the claim has the burden of proof. It is to say that he has the obligation to state quite precisely what he is talking about and to bring forward more evidence and tighter reasons than he might otherwise have been inclined to do. All argument is contextual, just as it is in law courts. Until an historian knows exactly what is being claimed and what would count for or against the claim, he can hardly do anything other than continue to insist that it seems unlikely or improbable.

The problem of assessment is at the heart of the problem of responsible belief and judgment. The logical difficulty with the appeal to uniqueness is that it undercuts all the formalities of argument that make assessment possible. A unique event is one which, by definition, is compatible with an indefinite range of contradictory assertions. Nothing counts for it and nothing against it. It is not only impossible to isolate data for such a claim or to employ warrants or to enter rebuttals but, most importantly, to qualify the conclusion in any respect. If, for example, a New Testament historian were to argue that a particular statement attributed to Jesus could not have been uttered by him because it clearly refers to a state of affairs after his time, another historian, believing in the uniqueness of Jesus, could easily argue that this uniqueness consisted precisely in his ability to foresee the future. The claim to uniqueness operates to destroy all of our normal warrants. It can thus be arbitrarily interjected at any point where a believer wants to keep critical inquiry at bay. It has, in fact, been used in just this way by fundamentalists with respect to the miracles. To argue that the resurrection belief is not arbitrary because it is the central claim of the New Testament is to beg the issue, for this judgment as to centrality is only possible by means of historical inquiry which presupposes just the kind of reasoning which the uniqueness claim calls into question. Almost all religions rest on such claims to uniqueness, and if they cannot all be true, the historian has no option but to go about his work with the canons which have made modern critical inquiry one of the monuments to the human spirit.

Moltmann advocates an historical method which attacks the historical understanding that works with analogy. Now if analogy is a rough way of referring to our normal canons of reasoning and inferring on the basis of present knowledge, I propose that Moltmann's approach is practically impossible. The best proof of this is Moltmann's attempt to interpret the resurrection appearances. For example, at one point he argues that although the actual raising of Jesus is without analogy and, therefore, not historically verifiable, we can verify who is involved in the alleged resurrection event. He means that we can verify that it was Jesus, rather than someone else, who appeared to the disciples. But how, we are certainly entitled to ask, could such a verification take place? Moltmann rests his case on the nature of the appearances of Jesus to the disciples. They were, it appears, vocatory visions in which the disciples recognized him.[24] "Without the speaking and hearing of words it would have been unlikely—indeed impossible—to identify the one who

24. *Ibid.*, p. 198.

appeared with the crucified Jesus. Without words spoken and heard the Easter appearances would have remained ghostly things. The appearances—for such things exist also in the history of religion—would have been taken as hierophanies of a strange, new heavenly Being, if they had not been coupled with the speaking of the one who here appeared."[25]

The ironic aspect of this argument is the way in which Moltmann, in order to clarify the nature of this unique event without analogies, is forced to appeal to just those non-unique, experiential connections between hearing and identification that enable us to grasp how the disciples could have recognized Jesus. But why is it necessary to do this if the event is utterly unique? When we are in the realm of the supernatural, anything is possible—or better, nothing need fit our categories of possibility—and the recognition of the disciples could as well have been effected by some means we cannot now imagine. Indeed, Moltmann even argues that it would have been *impossible* to recognize Jesus without the speaking and hearing of words. But by what right is Moltmann entitled to the category of the impossible when he has previously denied it to the secular historian? The idea only makes sense against the background of our present knowledge. Moltmann, in short, presupposes just what he denies. He trades on our ordinary (analogous?) reasoning from experience to warrant a judgment about an event to which it is said no analogies apply.

This contradiction naturally forces us back to a very naïve question: What exactly is it we are being asked to believe? For unless we know this we have no way of assessing the data, of examining the warrants, of entering a rebuttal, or of employing any kind of discriminatory judgment. The question is crucial for the historian but it is not lacking in theological significance. Indeed, to ask it casts into relief the dilemma of the "theology of hope." If the

25. *Ibid.*

SECULARISM, RESPONSIBLE BELIEF, AND THE "THEOLOGY OF HOPE"

Christian faith is built on a quite concrete event like a bodily resurrection, then the more concrete and specific is the hope in our own resurrection, because the more surely "resurrection" excludes alternative possibilities. But if the event is that unique that no analogies apply, then the greater the range of possible interpretations. The word resurrection, in this latter case, is worked loose from its soil in the concrete and becomes a symbol with a larger range of possible meanings. It can be regarded as a first-century way of trying to articulate a mystery of some sort. But what kind of mystery is it? Is it the continued personal existence of Jesus? Or is it a way of expressing the faith that Jesus' life had been so lived that its meaning could not be destroyed by his apparently meaningless death, that it had, so to speak, a future? Or is it a way of saying that God has judged Jesus' life and death to be of decisive significance, that he has seated Jesus "on the right hand"? Or is it a way of saying that the church is the resurrection body of the Lord? All of these interpretations have been offered at one time or another by theologians. I do not propose to defend one of them as the correct interpretation. I am only suggesting that once Moltmann concedes that we are dealing with an event for which there are no analogies, then it would seem that we no longer are bound to accept his particular translation of the symbol as the only one. A range of theological possibilities is open to us. Moreover, some of these theological possibilities involve no collision whatsoever with critical historical inquiry and require no tortured attacks on the modernity of the world. They do not deny the promise of hope, but they see this hope in quite different terms than Moltmann.

I wish to make it clear that I am not arguing that there is no legitimate use of the symbol "resurrection" or that there is no ground for an ultimate hope within Christian faith. I am, rather, calling attention to the fact that the contemporary Christian is quite aware that he is faced with a number of theological options and that it is precisely this diversity of interpretation that poses the problem of interpretation and belief. This, however, leads me to some further and final comments on the theological significance of this diversity and pluralism, which is to say, on the theological significance of secularism, for this pluralism is, I believe, but just another aspect of secularism and the problem it poses for theology.

III

In his Presidential Address to the Society for the Scientific Study of Religion,[26] Peter Berger argues that the crisis of belief which has given rise to the so-called secular theology can best be understood against the background of the pluralization of religious belief which is such a marked feature of Western culture in the last half-century. Christendom, he points out, developed and flourished in a situation in which the great majority of people lived with the same overall social structures and which the church as the sole "reality-defining institution" maintained and undergirded. This social situation was, to be sure, not entirely monolithic or lacking in internal strains. Nor was the church completely unaware of other competing religions or world wars. But for the most part, these were kept at a wide psychic and cultural distance, and not being able to find support in an institutional infra-structure, they never posed a fundamental threat to the socio-cultural and cognitive unity of Christendom.

The pathos of modern sensibility is that this cultural unity has been shattered and lost. As Berger points out, it is now impossible for any single institution to establish or maintain any monopoly in the definition of reality. "Instead, our situation is characterized by a market of world views, simul-

26. "A Sociological View of the Secularization of Theology," in *Journal for the Scientific Study of Religion*, VI, 1 (Spring 1967), pp. 3–16.

taneously in competition with each other. In this situation, the maintenance of any certitudes that go much beyond the empirical necessities of the society and the individual to function is very difficult indeed. Inasmuch as religion essentially rests upon superempirical certitudes, the pluralistic situation is a secularizing one and, *ipso facto*, plunges religion into a crisis of credibility."[27]

The assumption underlying Berger's analysis derives from the sociology of knowledge. It is that certitude of belief is largely a function of a socio-cultural situation. What men normally accept as unquestioned is grounded in specific social infra-structures that reflect communities of belief and interpretation. Knowing is inevitably tied to consensus and social corroboration. The explorations of linguistic analysts lend support to this sociological observation. They have pointed out that to say "I know" conveys an implied assurance that one's word is especially reliable because it has authority, which is to say, the credentials and backings for one's claims are regarded to be good. Good in this case means that they are commonly shared. To say "I believe" is often to say that one confidently regards something to be true but also is aware either that the shared reasons and backings do not justify the stronger "I know" or that these reasons and backing are not shared. When, however, someone finds that the reasons he gives for a claim are in basic conflict with those to whom he is speaking, a crisis of personal confidence will occur and both "I know" and "I believe" are difficult if not impossible for him to use.

As I have pointed out previously, one cannot speak of secularism as a phenomenon "out there," so to speak, in contrast with a pure and unified community of faith "in here." In previous eras, to be sure, the church did have a rough but recognizable sort of unity. It could speak to the world confidently because it had a sense of its own identity. This is no longer the case. Diversity and pluralism are now as characteristic of the church as of the so-called secular

27. *Ibid.*, p. 9.

world. There is no pristine community of Christian faith, if by this one means a consensus of doctrine, morality, or even a style of life. Men are not only confronted with the choice between Christianity and other world views; they are confronted with a choice among different versions of Christianity which, in turn, rest on differing interpretations of Scripture and of the tradition.

It is not necessary here to indicate the reasons for this diversity. However we explain it, any theology that aspires to be relevant must come to terms with it. Indeed, it could be argued that if one is interested in new tasks for theology, one of them might profitably be the appropriation, rather than the mere toleration, of pluralism and relativism and the adoption of a style that reflects what Karl Rahner calls the radical simplicity and the radical mystery of faith.[28]

Let me turn to this matter of theological style briefly, because it is not an unimportant factor so far as my own somewhat negative reaction to the "theology of hope" is concerned. The radical mystery of faith is, of course, a theme that occurs again and again in our Christian tradition. But it is a theme that acquires a new kind of relevance amidst our contemporary form of pluralization. As Karl Rahner has pointed out, the secularization of the world that has taken place in the last century or so has its parallel in what he calls the transcendentalization of the reflective consciousness of God,[29] which is to say, the awareness that God is the name for a radical mystery, the incomprehensible abyss underlying our existence. The secular man sometimes experiences this mystery but he is also aware how comic it is to dogmatize about it, especially when it is clear that no two theologians holding to the same revelation can even agree how to adjudicate their disputes about its interpretation.

The problem of the contemporary theologian as some of us see it is how to speak about this mystery without pre-

28. See his *Belief Today* (New York, 1967), chap. II.
29. *Ibid.*, p. 81.

tending to know more than one knows, to find a style of theological reflection that expresses the theologian's awareness that he lives at the edge of a great mystery which men will articulate differently. This reticence does not come easy to theologians in our generation because we have been weaned on theologies that profess to provide "The Christian Answer" to everything from psycho-neurosis to the most abstruse problems of metaphysics. We have too long regarded ourselves as village wise men who somehow or other possess a superior wisdom about God, science, the historical method, and the social and political problems of our time, not necessarily in that order. To confess that we do not have the answers to these issues will, no doubt, lose us a hearing with those who expect theologians to have this kind of certitude. It will certainly cut down on our honoraria at Religious Emphasis Weeks on university campuses, onto which we used to sail so confidently, deposit our theological cargoes, and then sail off again into the night before anyone could question us. But what we lose in honoraria we might gain in integrity, and that is not such a bad bargain for a theologian.

The distrust of the dogmatic temper in theology is not merely a matter of taste for some of us. We believe it to be close to the heart of faith itself. It is grounded in the conviction that God cannot be God except as the inconceivable and incomprehensible presence of grace. We are secularists enough that we become atheists when confronted with the heteronomous demand to believe propositions about the past or the future or about the mystery itself which are incompatible with the modes of thought we use to make sense out of our best and present experience. This is the most powerful religious insight we gained from the so-called neo-orthodox theology, and we will not easily surrender it. Barth, Bultmann, Tillich, and the Niebuhrs taught us that faith, whatever else it might be, is an inner liberation and that no man can be liberated by believing things which he inwardly does not understand to be true.

It seems clear that the mystery of faith and the simplicity of faith are closely related. The mystery of faith is the basis for the reticence of theology, for we know that we stand before that which is at the borders of language and thought. The simplicity of Christian faith is rooted in the conviction that living in relation to this mystery is what justifies human existence and sets men free.[30] It is this liberation which actually casts up and justifies the one hope without which we know we cannot live, the hope that we can experience this liberation again and again and so be set free to create and to love our neighbor. Mystery and simplicity function together as two sides of a theological Occam's Razor which slices through all the overbelief that theologians seem compelled to propagate. This Occam's Razor enables us to say something like this. Whatever else the Gospel may mean, all we can be sure of is that it means that it is possible for men to break out of the selfishness, the self-deceit, the arrogance which encrusts their lives and to live more selflessly, justly, honestly, and lovingly because they are confident that the whatever-it-is that underlies our existence, that gives and puts limits to our lives, is Holy and Good beyond all thought or imagination; that in the presence of this mystery all humanly accepted excellences, those things in which men put their confidence and trust, are childish.

The man of faith calls Jesus the Saviour not only because his life and death have the power, somehow, to call men to live in relation to this mystery but because when men commit themselves to his way, they find their existence altered and transformed in strange ways. They see things differently. What they once ignored, they now find to be of utmost importance. What they once regarded as folly,

---

30. To argue for the simplicity of faith and the Gospel is not the same thing as to argue for a cheap simplicity of theology. As Rahner points out, it may take a great deal of sophisticated theological reflection to establish the proper reference range for the symbols attached to the mystery or to make clear why it recedes from objectivizing thought. See *Theological Investigations,* vol. V (Baltimore, 1966), p. 36.

they now call wisdom, and what they once called wisdom now seems folly. The seemingly impersonal order that once impressed them as a sign of the utter indifference of the world they now see as the essential conditions of a life of freedom and responsibility, a sign of grace. What they once called the absurdity of being thrown into existence they now regard as the gift of life. What they once called the flux, the apparent random and meaningless succession of being upon being and event upon event, they now regard as the manifestation of an infinite and boundless power that takes delight in the sheer multiplicities of life and being. Everything the unbeliever points to as a sign of the utter indifference of the universe and, therefore, as a sanction for getting what one can out of this short, brutish life, the Christian regards as a sign of the Hidden One who glories in the richness of being and who calls men to a life of freedom and responsibility for the creation.

The Christian does not know how or why this transformation of vision occurs when he no longer trusts in himself and lives in relation to the mystery. He can only stammer words like "forgiveness" and "grace" and hope that these words are sufficiently useful to point to this new possibility of existing as a human being. But whatever he calls it, the Christian experiences something like inrushes of a new life, a new freedom and hope, and he looks back on his previous existence as a kind of half-life or, better, of half-death. He tries to grasp intellectually what has happened to him but it eludes his comprehension and understanding. Sometimes he doubts. All he can say for sure is that things seem different from what they once seemed and that they can also seem different to others and that this is Good News, a basis for hope. Hence, he becomes a steward of this mystery.

A theology which makes this radical mystery and simplicity of faith its prime object of concern will, I believe, be driven to a far more radical distinction between faith and the various expressions or articulations of faith, which

I shall call beliefs, than theology has hitherto been inclined to make, with one or two exceptions. Theology will need to distinguish between the *Urgeheimnis* and the attempts to embody this *Urgeheimnis* in language, which always reflects the historicity and the cultural relativity of the believer. This distinction is, of course, not a new one. But the implications of it lead to a kind of relativism and pluralism that no theologian in recent times, with the exception of H. Richard Niebuhr, has been willing to make the fundamental presupposition of his theological method. Niebuhr's "radical monotheism," which he always formulated with reticence and simplicity, was but the objective pole of a subjective relativism and pluralism. For when faith is attached to the One, it necessarily is aware of the relativity in knowledge and standpoint of the many. This is why Niebuhr could argue that it was possible to discern something like faith in the radical skepticism of the scientific community towards all claims to a final knowledge.[31] This "radical monotheism" was also the basis of Niebuhr's dislike of all Christocentrism. Not even Jesus, he argued, could be the final locus of the Christian hope. This is why he could not equate faith with any contingent belief or hope.

It is against this background that I can only register my conviction that the "theology of hope" cannot speak to the sensibility of our time. It is incompatible with the reticence that must characterize radical faith. It gives the impression, which Karl Rahner argues all theology should avoid, of "being better informed about God's absolute mystery and his intentions than is ever possible for a man, even with God's help."[32] This goes hand in hand with a theological posture which is uncomfortable with pluralism. It cannot acknowledge that other theological points of view are also possible ways of interpreting the faith. It attempts to pose the alternatives in the starkest terms; for example, we are

---

31. *Radical Monotheism and Western Culture* (New York, 1960), p. 86.
32. *Belief Today*, p. 83.

told that there are no genuine alternatives between a cosmological and anthropological theology.[33]

This brings me back to my observations on Moltmann's interpretation of the resurrection, with which I concluded the last section of this essay. His impatience with other points of view is, in part, a function of his having to impose a monolithic interpretation on the New Testament. No one can deny, of course, that the eschatological motif is a prominent one in much of the New Testament. But Moltmann leaves unexplored the significance of the fact that biblical criticism has disclosed that the New Testament is not a theological unity. There are fundamental theological differences among its various writers. The Protestant view of the infallibility of the Scriptures obscured this diversity, as have some of the more recent *Heilsgeschichte* theologians. The significance of this diversity is that theologians as different as Bultmann, on the one hand, and Moltmann, on the other, can both find support for their points of view in the New Testament. If Moltmann can support his case by interpreting Paul in a certain way and virtually ignoring the Fourth Gospel, Bultmann can interpret Paul in a different fashion and argue that the author of the Fourth Gospel sustained a systematic and full-scale assault on the idea of a future eschatological hope. Why is it necessary to deny that this diversity is inevitable? Pluralism is a fact, and the issue, I think, is how this diversity itself can be taken up into one's theological reflection. For myself, this diversity drives me back to reflection upon the mystery and simplicity of faith and the hope that resides in that faith. This point of view is not without its own problems, and it also is one among other possible theological interpretations. But unlike some of these other interpretations, it has the virtue, if it be such, of not requiring a conscious onslaught against the intellectual maturity of the modern secular world and its implicit ethic of belief.

33. Moltmann, see above, p. 6.

TOWARDS THE NEXT STEP IN THE DIALOGUE

Jürgen Moltmann

How can I best respond to a discussion just begun? I can only hope that my epilogue will serve as prologue to further transatlantic dialogue.

I

One problem of Christian theology today has been touched upon by practically all the contributors to this book. It is *the place of theology between the particular form of Christianity in the churches of a particular society and the universal form of Christianity as the "civil religion" (Robert Bellah) of this society*. In the United States theology exists concretely in the church seminaries and the religion departments of the colleges and universities. In the first instance it is taught relative to individual denominations and serves to a large extent the professional education of the ministry. In the second instance theology is by and large directed towards the University as a whole and more or less explicitly serves the civil religion. In Germany both tendencies of theological education coincide insofar as, with the exception of a few *Kirchliche Hochschulen,* faculties of theology only exist within the framework of the state universities. But the problems are rather similar.

This twofold *Sitz im Leben* of theology is mirrored in

the theoretical questions treated in this book. How is the origin of Christianity in Jesus Christ, represented in the biblical traditions, related to the present political responsibility of the Christian (Frederick Herzog)? How does the Christological grounding of hope tie in with its grounding in creation and the image of God in man (Harvey Cox)? How are God's special promise and his general providence related (Langdon Gilkey)? How can one represent Christian resurrection faith in accord with the canons of the secular historian (John Macquarrie)? Can we speak of an absolute character of the Christian faith in the modern context of a relativistic culture (Van A. Harvey)?

It is exactly in these fields of tension that Christian theology moves at all times, though always in very different ways. In my country and in my theological tradition the immediate and uncritical relationship of church and society, of Christian faith and civil religion, has been dissolved in the political events of our most recent history and the theology of the Confessing Church. All who have lived through the past epoch are suspicious and critical of a "theology of Christendom," implying a symbiosis of church and culture, throne and altar, religion and capital. This brought many theologians to a diastasis between church and society, theology and culture. They were looking for an exclusive "church theology" in order to find critical freedom over against society and politics. This movement, connected with the name Karl Barth, is often labeled neo-orthodoxy in America, although this is inadequate as far as Karl Barth's theology is concerned. It is in view of our historical experiences that a return to a naïve civil religion has become impossible. What is at stake in the more recent theological projects, such as "Revelation as History" (Wolfhart Pannenberg), "Theology of the World" (Johann Baptist Metz), and "Theology of Hope," is a critically responsible solidarity of the church with the dilemmas of society. While the naïve unity of church and society and theology and culture was followed by the diastasis between church and theology, on the one hand, and society and culture, on the other, today we are searching for a dialectical relationship between freedom and solidarity. It is, to use Hegel's terms, the dialectic of the relating and nonrelating of church and society, theology and culture. In this dialectic all critical negations are relational and not absolute.

My American partners, probably because of the close relationship between the Christian churches and civil religion in America, often understood these critical negations in an absolute sense as world-denying and science-opposing. I was surprised that only a few saw that I was trying to relate Christian theology critically to the negative and dangerous aspects of the modern world, that is, to the repressive structures of society and the increasing crisis aspect of modern civilization. Since this is a negative-critical relationship, most apparently got the impression that it was meant as the negation of all relationships, and they emphasized the religious experiences of the present. They stressed the significance of "natural theology," either with the aid of linguistic analysis, or Paul Tillich's ontology, or the neopositivist concept of science. In its place I wish to speak, with a special emphasis and qualification, of a "political theology." Since the Stoa it is regarded as a sister of "natural theology." For me it concretely affords the operational field of Christian theology. Christian theology must practically proceed in its thought processes in the area staked out by political relationships. But in order to remain free it dare not submit to the laws of this operational field. Christian theology must think and speak in the realm of the sciences and philosophy, but not under the categorial thought compulsions of this realm. Otherwise, it would have nothing to tell the world that the world could not tell itself.

Christian theology always moves between the historical particularity of its origins in the history of Jesus Christ and the eschatological universality of its goal. It cannot rid itself of the stigma of its historical particularity. Otherwise, it would lose every legitimation as *Christian* theology. Conversely, however, it must relate itself to the universal, the coming of God in his kingdom. Otherwise, it would lose its relevance as Christian *theology*. The relationship is indeed a dialectical one: Christians exist, act, suffer, and speak in the present, with the open Bible in their hands, as it were. Whoever closes the Bible in order to speak more effectively and contemporaneously no longer has anything new to tell his age. Whoever breaks off the conversation with the present in order to read the Bible more effectively finally merely engages in sterile monologues. Usually, for the *locus classicus* of a natural theology, one appealed to Rom. 1, 17 ff., so that one could relate Christian theology to law, cosmos, and everybody's conscience. Whenever I ponder these issues, I try to keep Rom. 8, 22 ff. in mind. I therefore wish to speak of a critical solidarity between Christians and non-Christians in "the sufferings of this present time" and of a companionship between Christians and all of creation in the "groaning in travail together." This "groaning" is not merely religious groaning, but also the suffering over the concrete economical, social, and political misery of mankind.

II

Today the *question of God* again arises in theology with special urgency. Frederick Herzog, Harvey Cox, and Langdon Gilkey raised critical questions about my eschatological view of the reality of God. Van A. Harvey offered as alternative an anthropological model for understanding transcendence. Since the appearance of the death of God theology the question of God has again moved into the center of theological reflection in Europe as well as in America. I would like to try to illumine my affirmations on the *Deus qui futurus est* with some philosophical reflections.

It is a fact that I arrived at an eschatological understanding of the reality of God and of the experience of God *in hope* on grounds of biblical theology. But biblical theology was not examined in greater detail. I therefore turn to philosophical theology. The turn to *theology as eschatology* can also be shown up as a possible and meaningful turn on grounds of philosophical theology. It is not an issue of the German tradition of appealing to an *immune* authority of "the Word," as Langdon Gilkey assumed. The authority of "the Word" proves itself first of all in that it becomes the author of new possibilities in reality. This has nothing to do with traditionalism, biblicism, or clericalism and its authoritarian understanding of the Word. But it also has nothing to do with religious liberalism for which "the Word" of Christian proclamation is a merely symbolic expression for already available experiences.

Christian God-talk has for a long time oriented itself in the metaphysical model of transcendence. A metaphysical understanding of the reality of God, however, is valid only so long as the reality of the world is understood physically. Since Aristotle, "physics and metaphysics" form a unity. Therefore, the medieval tradition understood the reality of God in accordance with Aristotelian metaphysics and the reality of the world in keeping with Aristotelian physics. In this framework Christian theology merged the biblical tradition and the church tradition of God with the metaphysical concept of God of the *prima philosophia* of all sciences. With the change in "physics," that is, in the experience of the world and the understanding of reality, the "metaphysical" understanding of God also changed of necessity.

Since the beginning of the modern age the model of "physics and metaphysics" has been replaced by the model of "existence and transcendence." Modern man no longer views himself as a part of nature and the cosmos, but rather, conversely, he understands the world as the field of his constructive possibilities in science and technology. He sees himself as *maître de la nature* (Descartes). No longer does the heaven of metaphysics unlock for him the physics of the earth, but his own transcendental subjectivity opens the world for him. Therefore, in the modern age, transcendence is more and more experienced as inner dimension of human subjectivity and intersubjectivity. In following Rudolf Bultmann, this is probably what Van A. Harvey had in mind.

In the modern society of the large, non-transparent industrial systems, however, this model of "existence and transcendence" has become impotent, since modern man is by no means a free Lord of his creations, but has become the slave of his own works, his organizations and bureaucracies. Although the inner relationship of the self to the *Urgeheimnis* (Van A. Harvey) may free man inwardly, it does not create a free society as a matter of course. This inner consciousness of faith functions rather as comfort for the soul or escape mechanism in the midst of inhuman conditions which, described as "pluralism" or "secularization," are merely covered up ideologically.

If today one understands the reality of man and his world as "history" and by "history" means to point to the present tension between necessity and freedom, life and death, person and society, subjectivity and thingification, where then does one experience transcendence? If we initially translate the old models, one could say: the way metaphysics related to physics, and transcendence to existence, eschatology relates to "history." "Eschatology" in a certain sense is "metahistory." In the present conflicts and polarizations which are experienced as history, one asks for the meaning and the goal of history. "Eschatology" is the realm of ends, visions, hopes, and fears, in which the sense and nonsense of history is decided upon. This realm is a "space ahead" (Ernst Bloch) towards which one transcends historically. In a general sense, it is "the future." But eschatology implies a *last* future. It speaks not only of "future history," but also of a "future of history." Eschatological future, therefore, characterizes not only the constant transcending of an historical present into the next, but also a transcendence for that immanence which as a whole is called "history." It appears to me that one can say in somewhat general terms of the phenomenology of religion that today transcendence is experienced more and more as historical boundary of the future. Where one finds critical perspectives in facing the strife of the present and new tendencies towards change and renewal, where promises and hopes emerge that transcend the present antagonisms in the direction of peace, there transcendence is experienced and practiced in the act of transcending. Already in the transition from the model of "physics and metaphysics" to the modern model of "existence and transcendence" many had the feeling that "God is dead." Actually, however, it was merely the boundary of the experience of God that had changed.

Perhaps we stand today at the crossroads of a new transition to new experiences of transcendence, only that some do not use the word "God" for them as yet because it is tied up with the previous models. The discussion of my project of an eschatological understanding of God in present reality was carried on in the old grooves of the metaphysical debate about theism and alienated my formulations from their intrinsic intentions. I must, however, accept the criticism that for the molding and formulating of a new eschatological experience of God I did not use words of modern poets, but the ancient biblical language, which speaks of Exodus and promise, of resurrection and parousia. There are two reasons for this merging of biblical theology with modern tendencies of historical reflection. First, I think that in the modern situation one can find new impulses in the older Christian and Old Testament traditions of hope for the coming God, in order not merely to articulate certain experiences, but also to experience new things. Second, I believe that Christian theology has the responsibility to join the biblical tradition with the spirit of the present future, since, otherwise, we would have to give up being Christian, or stop talking about God, transcendence, and eschatology.

III

Together with the question of God, the question of *the uniqueness of the Christian faith* is raised with equal urgency. Christians believe in God because of Jesus and in Jesus because of God. Their faith in God is grounded in the history of Jesus Christ and shaped by it. At the beginning of the Christian faith stands the confession of the God who raised Jesus from the dead, and the confession of the crucified Jesus, who through the resurrection was made "the Christ of God" (cf. Rom 10, 9). In the history of Jesus Christ, concentrated in his "twofold end" (M. Kähler), God is revealed for Jesus' sake and Jesus for God's sake.

While in primitive Christianity the offense and the foolishness of the Christian faith was seen in God's revelation in and through a crucified one, the offense and the foolishness of the Christian faith in the modern age has shifted to the historical undergirding of the resurrection faith. The difficulties today lie between "the historian and the believer" (Van A. Harvey). Van A. Harvey and John Macquarrie critically examined especially my reasoning about the Christian hope for the coming God in the resurrection of Jesus Christ. Since the beginning of historical criticism Christian theology has been engaged in battles of retreat. One evaded the historical question by letting the Christian faith migrate from theoretical reason to settle down in practical reason. Kant's "moral faith of reason" has become the most travelled way out. But already Kant no longer wanted to call that faith which the critique of pure reason still allowed "Christian" faith. Accordingly, in Van Harvey's constructive reflections about "the radical mystery of faith," any Christological underpinning of this faith disappears. "Radical monotheism" replaces the so-called "Christocentrism." By this move he finds it possible to let "the radical mystery" of the subjective faith peacefully coexist with the pluralism and the secularity of the world of the modern university, but loses thereby also any legitimation to call this faith mystery "Christian." Jesus thus can neither be called the ground, nor the Lord of such a faith.

One can also evade the historical question in such a way that one divides up history into a horizontal and a vertical history. Here the cross and the resurrection of

Jesus only function significantly in the vertical history between God and man. They thus belong to the "divine history" and touch the horizontal world history with its cause-effect concourse only tangentially or symbolically. This divine history then proves itself in its "meaning content" not through another reality, but through itself alone. Karl Barth is usually understood in this sense. Also here the Christian faith can coexist with any scientific view of history. Apparently, Hans Frei sees herein a possibility to let the neo-positivist historicism coexist with Karl Barth's revelation theology.[1] Non-positivist and non-pure empiricist concepts of history appear to him, therefore, as "ideological." Here the Christian hope is indeed "grounded" Christologically. But, practically, how should it get at least one of its feet on the ground, seeing that it has left the earth, its horizontal history, so far behind? How should Christian faith become practical, if it has already immunized itself against any check?

The third possibility to try to tackle the problem of faith and history consists initially in the plain effort no longer to evade the problem, but together with the historian to lock horns in the battle for the one truth on the battlefield of actual history. For the problems, the temptations, and the contentions only emerge if the Christian faith clings to the history that creates it and if the Christian hope joins the vision of God with the vision of the goal of history. The one is linked to the other. Here the believer does not see facts other than those that the non-believer can also see, but he sees another coherence of meaning. If the Christian faith, as long as it is *Christian* faith, presupposes historical recollection of Jesus' history and the Christ event, it does not demand a sacrifice of the intellect. The resurrection event of the crucificial Jesus, in terms of the understanding of the resurrection accounts as well as in terms of the insight of the neutral historian, is an occurrence *sui generis* and without analogy in the same category. For the historian,

1. In his review of the *Theology of Hope, Union Seminary Quarterly Review*, 33:3 (Spring, 1968), pp. 267 ff.

who seeks to grasp the meaning of an event on grounds of a comparison with other events in history in accord with the principle of analogy, this event becomes meaningless. Only from the history of its effect in the believers and in the church can the historian arrive at some understanding of this event.

For the believer, the resurrection event, which is proclaimed to him, since it opens the future, becomes an analogy-creating and history-producing event. Also, the believer sees in history no analogies of the event in the same category. The resurrection faith has never claimed that resurrections happen always, everywhere, and at all times. It has always maintained that only Jesus has been freed from the history of death, but not we. For the Christian faith, the resurrection of the Crucified One becomes the ground of hope in the life that overcomes death. If in the history of death there are no analogies of Jesus' resurrection, there are at least analogies in the category of the Spirit and his effects. For us today, the experienceable form of the resurrection is "the Spirit of the resurrection" or "the power of the resurrection." It is the justification of the godless in a world of unrighteousness, the experience of faith certainty in the midst of uncertainty, the experience of love in the midst of death. Also, the movements of renewal in Christian history in Renaissance, Reformation, and Revolution are spirit of this Spirit. The conflict between believers and non-believers can therefore not end in the believer's defenseless retreat to a storm-and-stress-free place immune against all critique, but on the field of history must turn into his battling through with the ideologies and with positivism the battle for truth. If his historical reasoning and his historical hope are subjected to critique, he himself must also subject the presuppositions and interests of the non-believers, the ideologists and positivists, to his critique. Whoever regards this as "animosity towards science" apparently does not know any too well the internal questionableness of the sciences and their involvement with the interests of modern society.

I am surprised that Van A. Harvey, in good Teutonic

form, as it were, so vigorously attacks the resurrection faith in my theology with the help of "carbon-14-historicism," while in his book on *The Historian and the Believer* he has held that the resurrection faith is "the right understanding of Jesus." Why is the faith that Jesus calls forth qualified as resurrection faith? If the resurrection faith is the right understanding of Jesus, how does this faith understand God? Apparently, not as innocuous name for the "abyss of existence," but as the power that in the history of death opens for man a final and definite future. If the resurrection faith is "the right understanding of Jesus," how then does this faith understand the world? Apparently, not relativistically as country club for all possible games of culture, but as battlefield between God and the idols, the powers of life and the agents of death, peace and anxiety, Christ and Anti-Christ. In our contemporary, rather apocalyptic, situation, I will spare myself the concretizing of this view of reality "as history." While it is true that the historian always works in limited areas of history with limited methods, especially when he works analytically, he nevertheless always reaches points where he encounters the abyss of history which by no means is God, but the destructive *nihil*. Where this nothing, this absurdity, this abolute death encounters him, he has an "experience of history," the way everyone who is involved in history can have it every day. Here arises the question of the meaning and the meaninglessness of world history. It is not answered by history itself. The Christian resurrection faith in the coming God, born of the cross, begins in such experiences to speak of history. "We are first of all historical beings before we are contemplators of history, and only because we are historical beings do we turn into the latter" (Wilhelm Dilthey). It occasionally helps to remind oneself of this relationship between suffering history and knowing history, between the practice of history and its theory, so that the discussion of the resurrection faith does not become too banal.

Notes on Contributors

HARVEY COX received his B.A. from the University of Pennsylvania, B.D. from Yale Divinity School, and Ph.D. from Harvard. He is Professor of Church and Society at Harvard Divinity School, and author, most recently, of *The Feast of Fools.*

LANGDON GILKEY received his B.A. from Harvard, and Ph.D. from Columbia and Union Theological Seminary. He is Professor of Theology at the University of Chicago, and author, most recently, of *Shantung Compound.*

VAN A. HARVEY received his B.A. from Occidental College, B.D. from Yale Divinity School, and Ph.D. from Yale University. He is Professor of Religious Thought at the University of Pennsylvania, and author of *The Historian and the Believer.*

FREDERICK HERZOG has studied at the University of Bonn and the University of Basel, and received his Th.D. from Princeton Theological Seminary. He is Professor of Systematic Theology at Duke Divinity School, and the author of *Understanding God.*

JOHN MACQUARRIE received his B.D. from Trinity College, Glasgow, and M.A. and Ph.D. from Glasgow University. He is Professor of Systematic Theology at Union Theological Seminary. Among his most recent works are *God-Talk* and *A Dictionary of Christian Ethics*.

JÜRGEN MOLTMANN received his Th.D. from the University of Göttingen, and has taught at the universities of Göttingen and Bonn. He is Professor of Systematic Theology at the University of Tübingen, and the author of *The Lordship of Christ and Human Society* and *Religion, Revolution, and the Future,* as well as *Theology of Hope.*